Prais

Vivian Arend

"If you've never read a Vivian Arend book you are missing out on one of the best contemporary authors writing today."
~ *Book Reading Gals*

"Vivian Arend takes us on a sensual ride as Mitch and Anna explore her sexuality... From beginning to end this story is very hot and highly entertaining.
~ *Where the Night Kind Roam*

"Brilliant, raw, imaginative, irresistible!!"
~ Avon Romance

"This story will keep you reading from the first page to the last one. There is never a dull moment..."
~ *Landy Jimenez*

"I loved Mitch and Anna. Their chemistry was off the charts and it wasn't so much what they did that made it so hot (though it helped) it was the way they did it. If the Six Pack Ranch Series is as hot as this was, I'll definitely being going back to read it."
~ *Lost in a Book*

"This was my first Vivian Arend story, and I know I want more! "
~ *Red Hot Plus Blue Reads*

"HOLY FREAKIN' HELL IS THIS HOT!!!"
~ *Book-A-Holic Anon*

Also available from Vivian Arend

~*CONTEMPORARY TITLES*~

Six Pack Ranch
Rocky Mountain Heat
Rocky Mountain Haven
Rocky Mountain Desire
Rocky Mountain Angel
Rocky Mountain Rebel
Rocky Mountain Freedom

Thompson & Sons
Rocky Ride
One Sexy Rid
Let It Ride
A Wild Ride

Adrenaline Search & Rescue
High Risk
High Passion
High Seduction

Turner Twins
Turn It Up
Turn It On

DreamMakers
All Fired Up
Love Is A Battlefield
Don't Walk Away

~*~

A full list of Vivian's paranormal print titles
is available on her website
www.vivianarend.com

Rocky Ride

Vivian Arend

This is a work of fiction. Names, characters, places, and incidents either are the product of the author's imagination or are used fictitiously, and any resemblance to any persons, living or deal, business establishments, event, or locales is entirely coincidental.

Rocky Ride
Copyright 2014 by Vivian Arend
ISBN: 978-1-497349-63-6
Edited by Jorrie Spencer
Cover by Angela Waters
Proofed by Sharon Muha

Chapter One

September, Rocky Mountain House

HEAT ROLLED along her spine, leaving a sticky residue behind like at the conclusion of a long shift on an endless summer day. Only it wasn't hard labour that had brought the undeniable flush to her skin. It wasn't the sweltering breeze blowing past, causing leaves on the nearby trees to tremble, or the scalding sun beating down on her dash.

It was sex. Or more accurately, the *anticipation* of sex.

A straight-up, body-pounding, muscle-clenching fuck about to be delivered with all too much finesse by her favourite speeder in the entire district.

Right now she wasn't in the RCMP cruiser, and she certainly wasn't on any major highway in the Rocky Mountain House area. Anna Coleman sat in her personal vehicle at the side of a lonely country gravel road as *anticipation* rapidly rolled toward *consummation*.

Thank God.

Her side-view mirror gave her a flawless view of Mitch Thompson. He uncurled himself from his Harley, removed his helmet and left it behind on the handlebars. Her heart rate kicked up as he sauntered closer, dragging a hand through his dark hair before pulling off his sunglasses and hanging them from his front pocket. Black leathers gripped his thighs, sunlight flicking off the fabric as he strode forward. The tight black T-shirt only emphasized the width of his chest and biceps, the dark lines of his tattoos curling over his forearms to where they ended in ragged flames on his wrists and the back of his hands.

Hmmm, his hands...

His usual cocky grin was absent, instead his expression one of total dignity and control, one step away from a glare. From this distance, she couldn't see the golden specks in his dark brown eyes, but they were there, the knowledge of how they flashed brighter during moments of intense pleasure intimately embedded in her memory. His hair was too short to be more than rumpled from the time under his helmet, the dark brown strands matching the shadow of facial hair darkening his square jawline.

Nice. Today Mitch was one hundred percent hoodlum playing one hundred percent dangerous authority, and the combination caused one hundred and ten wicked reactions. She squeezed her knees together, but the pressure did nothing to ease the localized ache between her thighs.

He rapped his knuckles on her window.

Anna moved slowly, as if she hadn't been panting for this moment. She rolled down her window but stared straight ahead, refusing to make eye contact.

2

"I need to see some identification," he drawled.

"What seems to be the problem?" she tossed back, one side of her mouth twitching upward briefly before she got her amusement under control.

"You have no idea what you've done?" Mitch leaned in, elbows resting on the doorframe and inhaled deeply. "You got an explanation for the smell in here?"

She jerked to face him. That question wasn't in their usual repartee. "*Smell?*"

His panty-melting grin exploded. "*Hmm*. Like sweet, hungry pussy."

Holy moly. Anna squirmed. "You're mistaken. I'm not transporting any animals."

"Get out of the vehicle. Now." He jerked her door open.

Anna was in no hurry. Drawing out the tease, taunting him for a moment or two could only heighten the experience for them both. Make what was sure to follow that much more explosive.

Pleasure licked around her as she obediently stood beside her car, his gaze skimming over the curve of her breasts. Lower, over her hips, lingering on the length of legs left exposed by her short miniskirt. She'd strapped on high heels, not much more than bits of buttery soft leather wrapped around five-inch spikes, and he swore lightly at the sight of them, fiery red against the dull grey gravel.

Screw it if the stilettos were impractical. This was her fantasy, and for the next half hour she'd damn well wear what she wanted.

A growl escaped Mitch as she pushed him to the edge of control. He squatted, one finger tracing the line of leather around her ankle and up the back of her calf to tease the sensitive skin behind her knee. "You have a license for those weapons?"

"Maybe. Maybe not."

The passion in his eyes burned as he glanced upward. "Hands against the car."

Anna glanced around cautiously as she twisted to obey. Double-checking there were no farmers using the remote shortcut to move bailers or haul hay from field to shed. Nothing to break the mood. No observers.

Although in theory the idea of being watched wasn't unwelcome, getting caught playing kinky sex games in public with Mitch Thompson would not be a good thing.

He stepped behind her, heat increasing as the space between them narrowed. He patted her down, efficiently, quickly, but even the brief contact was enough to drive a moan from her lips.

"You like that, do you?" he growled. "Bet you're hiding things from me."

"Maybe," she repeated, closing the distance to make contact between their hips. Her ass bumped his groin, and his hard-on digging into her butt just made things that much hotter. "You'd better check. Thoroughly."

"Strip search." His hands slipped over her hips, one dropping to cup her sex, the other up past her breasts to rest lightly over her throat. His lips hovered only inches from her ear, close enough the scruff on his chin and cheeks scratched her skin. "You get me so damn hot I'm ready to rip your clothes off and fuck you right here," he confessed.

Anna rubbed them together again, all too pleased at the tormented sound she dragged from him. "No need to rip anything," she panted.

Mitch bunched her skirt under his fingers, cursing loudly as he met nothing but bare skin. Totally bare.

"Sweet fuck, you shaved."

"Waxed. Oh *God*, don't stop."

He'd slipped his fingers over her pussy, delving between her labia to get his fingers wet before circling her clit. "Bare pussy. Wet bare pussy. Jesus *fuck*, woman. You think I can just stick my cock in you, and be done?"

"Good by me," she insisted. No need to stop for condoms either—thank God for clean health records and efficient birth control. A gasp escaped as he pushed a finger deep inside. "Mitch, just do me already."

He twirled her, his eyes blazing with lust as he pushed her shoulders against the car. "No."

He took her lips before she could protest, kissing her like he did damn near everything. High speed, high intensity, igniting high-octane flames that lit her inside and out. His tongue licked into her mouth, his fingers cleverly undoing the elastic that had held her hair in a neat ponytail. She wrapped her arms around his neck in the hopes of keeping him close. It was no use, though, as he pulled away far too soon and put his teeth to her neck, a hand slipping between them to resume tormenting her clit with a steady rhythm.

"Don't taunt me," Anna begged. "I was ready for sex five minutes after you called me this morning."

"Hmm. You've been hot and aching all day?"

Another round of skillfully applied pressure slid over her clit, and her hips jerked involuntarily. "Aching so hard."

"Did you play with yourself?" he asked, easing off slightly, his thumb pulsing in a faint unending beat. "Did

5

you have to hide somewhere so you could slip your fingers into your panties? Did you think about me shoving my cock deep inside you again and again until you scream?"

"Yes," she hissed.

Mitch pulled back, and she whimpered in protest. She reached for him, but he shook his head, that evil grin back in place as he eased away far enough he could leer at her. "Show me," he demanded.

There was no ignoring the command, and hell if she wanted to. At this point, if he wasn't going to deal with her…

He dropped to his knees so as she slid her fingers down to touch herself, his head was only inches away. She stroked lightly to stop from bursting into flames in under three seconds.

"Give me your hand," Mitch ordered.

She held it out, and he caught her wrist, licking her fingers one at a time. The rough contrast of his tongue over the pads of her fingers teased her senses. He moved her hand, and she shook, leaning harder on the car to stop from melting to the ground as he used her own wet fingers to play with her clit. Slipping between her folds and stroking her to a feverish pitch.

"Mitch, please." Begging came all too easy at this point. "Give me your cock."

"Come first. Come on my tongue." He put his lips to her pussy, driving his tongue deep, fucking her with it as he worked her fingers over her clit again and again.

A long, low cry flowed from her lips, trembling in the air like the nearby leaves as the first wave of her orgasm hit her. Hips bucking forward, aching for something to hold, her pussy contracted and she called out his name.

He was on his feet, zipper down, cock in hand. She stared through sex-hazed eyes at the momentary glint as the ball bearings adorning his cock head shone in the sunlight. He hitched her thigh over his hip, her skirt bunched around her waist.

"Hold on, this is going to be a wild ride," Mitch promised.

He put the head of his cock to her pussy and thrust upward. One motion, another. It took three drives for him to work all the way in, her climax still rippling around him.

Then the fucking began in earnest.

Mitch leaned over her, holding under her thigh to keep her wide open, his other hand under her ass, protecting her as he pounded in deep. Hard.

Incredibly intense and vivid, and like always, Anna came alive. This was what she craved—this bright place of indulgence and passion. Every nerve on high alert, every motion a spark leading to the next level of pleasure.

"God, so tight around my cock. You're squeezing me like a vise. You like fucking out here, don't you? My cock drilling you in two."

"Oh, *yes.*"

Mitch growled again and thrust harder. "Dirty girl. Bare-ass-naked under your skirt. Sun shining down on us—hell, anyone could drive up right now, couldn't they?"

Anna shuddered.

"Hmm, yeah. They'd see you, legs open wide, pussy wet for my cock." Mitch caught her by the chin and kissed her like a mad man as he fucked hard for another dozen strokes.

VIVIAN AREND

Sensory overload was setting in. It wasn't just his
cock. Or his touch, or his teeth digging into her neck. It
was the words and the place and the...

"Oh God, *oh*..."

His piercing got her again, a cascade breaking from
deep within where he'd been stroking her unmercifully
with the damn thing. She had no chance of stopping a
second climax from ripping free, especially with a thick,
satisfying length of cock to squeeze around this time.

"Fuck *yes*, come on my cock, babe. That's it. Fuck me
hard," Mitch ordered.

He shoved his hand between them and caught her
clit. Anna screamed, all restraint vanishing as she came,
liquid shooting from her pussy to coat his hand, his legs.
Pressure escaped in spurts, her spine melted, and
pleasure turned her limbs molten.

Numbing pleasure, incredibly intense. "Oh my *God*,
oh *my God*."

She'd breathe later, she decided. Right now there
was too much happening between her legs to bother with
incidentals like air to her lungs and blood to her brain.

"Jesus *fuck*, yeah. Damn." Mitch buried himself deep
and came, his body crushing her to the car as his hips
pulsed helplessly, face contorted with extreme pleasure.
Anna watched as long as she could, but white spots hung
before her eyes and it was so much simpler to close them
and let Mitch support her.

A breeze surrounded them, cooling air pushed over
heated limbs. Her heart rate slowed enough that the
buzz of tiny insects in the trees and the distant motors of
farm equipment became audible again. Mitch held her in
place, both feet off the ground with her bare ass pressed
against the car window, and in the middle of the languid

8

sensation controlling her body, the image struck her as hilariously funny.

Mitch breathed slowly before finding his voice. "What's making you laugh?"

Her world was still spinning. "I think I just left an ass print on my window."

MITCH PULLED his brain back from the faraway place sex had sent it and let an evil chuckle free at her wry comment. "Good thing this isn't your cruiser. I'd like to see you explain questionable prints to Nick."

"Oh man, that would not go over well." Anna ran her fingers through Mitch's hair, pushing the short length upright over his forehead. "My partner would make me fill out cleaning and sterilization forms in triplicate."

Mitch leaned in to kiss her tenderly while she remained in the soft and lazy post-sex mood. She wouldn't allow him to pet her for long, so he took every chance he could to savour the bits of time he did get.

Anna sighed happily as he nuzzled her neck. His cock was still in her pussy—he'd be happy to stay there for the rest of the day, but if this was like any previous time, in a couple of minutes Anna would start the process of withdrawing from him. Withdrawing from who she was when she was with him.

He'd bite his tongue like usual and let her. This time. But the day was coming when he wasn't going to let it slide. A day really soon.

"You're a dangerous man, Mitch Thompson," Anna muttered. "It's a good thing I have a change of clothes in the trunk. Sorry about your leathers."

"As if I'm going to complain I made you come so hard you got me wet." He couldn't hide the gloating in his voice.

"It's your piercing. Hits me just right, and you know it." Anna wriggled, and he reluctantly lowered her thigh, slowly separating them. A rush of semen and lingering moisture from her explosive orgasm ran down her leg. "God, I need not only a change of clothes, but a shower."

Mitch grinned harder, pushing her against the car before she could run away and clean up the signs of their wild debauchery. He pinned her in place, his hands pushing her wrists to the roof as he slid one leg between her thighs and held her bare ass to the car door. Her dark brown hair was a mess tumbled about her shoulders, her pupils still full and dark against her pale blue irises. The flush on her cheeks from the wild sex, not some maidenly blush. "I like you dirty," he admitted.

Her eyes flashed brightly for a second before she pulled on her cop uniform. Not the navy slacks and powder-blue shirt, but the mental shield she wore. As real as a tangible piece of fabric, Anna transformed before his eyes from his sexy, uninhibited lover to the woman who wrote up tickets and toed the line.

All the lines. All the time.

"I need to go, Mitch. My parents are having the family over for dinner, and since I'm not on duty, I'm heading over early."

Mitch paused before doing the only thing he could— he let her free.

He put his cock back in his pants, adjusting carefully before zipping. Anna moved to her trunk, intensely focused on anything but him, it seemed. She used a bunch of wet wipes to clean up. Pulled on a pair of plain, serviceable panties and covered them with faded jeans. Her footwear was switched for practical runners.

She scooped up her fuck-me high heels by the leather straps and let them dangle in the air, staring at them with a tortured expression.

Did she know how easily he read her at these moments?

"Anytime you want to wear those shoes, I'm down with it," he teased softly.

She jerked upright, shaking her head briskly. "It's a good thing I don't really have anywhere to go while wearing them. Doubt I could walk more than three feet without falling on my ass."

She shoved them into a grey duffle bag, along with the miniskirt. Hiding away all signs of who she was. What she liked. A wave of frustration rolled through him, and Mitch opened his mouth...

And just as quickly closed it again.

Not the time. Not the place, but soon.

Damn soon if he had his way.

She finally made eye contact as she opened her car door. Quiet, impersonal, with a faint smile like you'd give to an acquaintance you spotted at the supermarket. "Talk to you later?"

"No problem. You know where to find me." He eased back, arms crossed over his chest as she got in and drove away.

Drove away, and took his fucking heart with her.

In one way it was hilarious. Mitch Thompson had fallen hopelessly in love with the worst possible woman in town—one fighting tooth and nail against letting her real nature free.

He stared after her polite, serviceable car as she headed home to her traditional family dinner. She'd peel the potatoes and set the table, and afterward, she'd help her mother wash the dishes while her brothers and father talked about the ranch chores and fields and crops.

The contrast between what she'd be doing in an hour and what they'd just done haunted Mitch. Not the actual sex, but her attitude. There was nothing wrong with an old-fashioned family gathering, but the Anna he'd been savouring wasn't someone she showed to anyone else.

For the past two months, since Anna had given in to the heat between them, they'd been meeting on the sly. Playing games and finding pleasure in trying every sexual thing she suggested. Mitch had reached the point where sex was no longer enough.

That fire he'd witnessed all too often in her eyes? Her evil sense of humour and dirty imagination? He longed to have those things turned on him all the time, not only during clandestine moments. He wanted to stop seeing her shove her real needs into a damn duffle bag as she hid her sexy self away. His frustrations boiled as he stared after her.

One of her taillights blinked red.

For fuck's sake—she'd used her turn signal at the first intersection. Two gravel roads leading from nowhere to nowhere, not a soul around for miles, and she still flipped on the damn indicator.

And there it was. The perfect example of what was wrong, and what needed to change. She was so used to following rules for the sake of following rules she'd forgotten to choose what was going to make her really happy.

The woman had a respectable career and an orderly life, and boned him on the side as long as no one knew. How long did she think that would be enough for either of them?

Mitch pulled on his helmet and settled onto his bike, ready to burn off his anger on the highway before heading home.

They weren't that much different, Anna Coleman and himself. His days of being someone's dirty little secret were over. Her days of hiding her real self away were drawing to an end as well.

Now he had to find a way to make that happen.

Chapter Two

IF ENDLESS tedium was the nearest thing to hell on earth, Nick Dowes seemed determined to hasten its arrival. Around the table at RCMP headquarters, the staff were trapped in their seats as Anna's partner headed into his third page of suggestions to streamline operations.

The concepts were good, the delivery mind-numbing. Anna's phone vibrated, and she lowered her gaze to the screen hidden in her lap.

What U doing?

Being bored silly, but she couldn't text that to Mitch. She *wouldn't* text that—frustrations with her job in general and her coworker in particular were not something she would share with anyone. Not only would it be unprofessional, there was not much use in sharing when she couldn't change things.

"I'm sure we can all see why this would create an increase in efficiency…"

One ear on Nick, Anna texted back. *In meeting*

Boring

Anna suppressed a snort. *What's up?*

This was about the time he'd usually contact her to arrange their next get-together, and good grief, did she need it.

Have an idea. Call when you're done work

Oh, she liked where this was going. *Secrets?*

Nice secrets, he texted. *Later*

The thrill of the unknown shouldn't have made her entire body come alive. A simple text message, and she was ready to track down Mitch Thompson and crawl all over him.

She didn't want to analyze the desire. Didn't want to justify it, but she'd willingly admit her obsession with the man was real.

"Anna."

A deep voice broke through her distraction, and she whipped her head up to spot her commanding officer staring. Damn. Had she been caught? She slipped her phone into her pocket, adrenaline blasting through her veins and helping her focus.

"Yes, sir?"

He'd moved to the head of the table, taking over for Nick—*thank God*—and resumed control of the meeting. "I've gotten a request from the high school for an officer liaison, and I'd like to put you down for the duty."

Her stomach fell. "Me, sir?"

"I'd love to take that role," Nick cut in. "With the extra training I did this summer, I'm up to date on youth issues."

Staff Sergeant Max paused then shook his head. "Your training is good, but I think Anna is a better match for the school. It would do all the students good to see a

15

woman in a position of authority. No, unless you have any serious concerns about the posting, Constable Coleman, I'll get you the contact information for the school. You can arrange with the guidance counselor for the best way to work this task into your shifts."

No serious concerns other than she didn't want the job, but she wasn't about to admit that. "If you feel it's in the best interest of the department, of course. I'll take the position."

Nick settled in the chair across from her, lining up his file folders with deliberate care as he avoided meeting her gaze.

Great. Not only did she have a work-enforced mandate to go hang out with teens—her second least-favorite population group after babies and toddlers—her partner was acting as if she'd kicked a kitten. Maybe her being away at times was going to mess with "efficiency" or something.

She left the room as soon as they were dismissed, grabbing her gear and heading for the cruiser. She had highway patrol for the rest of the afternoon. With the mood she was in? God help her brothers if she caught one of them speeding.

"Anna, wait up," Nick called after her.

She paused with a hand on her car door, a deepening sense of guilt rolling through her. They'd been partnered together for nearly a year, and she still didn't feel much of a connection with him. In their area, partners didn't mean 24/7 working together, but most times when they were assigned two-man duties she was hooked up with Nick.

What was wrong with her that she couldn't make that deep association with him that others talked about having with their partners? The two of them worked together fine, only...beyond the job? Nothing. Less than nothing.

Nick ran up, his blond hair neatly tucked under his hat. Every button and bow in place. "I need a minute of your time."

She pasted on her friendliest smile. "You need a hand with something?"

He waved off her offer. "Just wanted to make sure you know, if down the road you decide to drop the liaison position, I'd appreciate you putting forward my name as a replacement."

His attitude was all sunshine and roses now, instead of the annoyance she spotted earlier. "I'll keep that in mind," she promised.

He was gone before she could make any small talk, which only added to her frustration. Partner. *Ha.* More like *person she worked with whom she still knew zero about.*

She hit the highway, heading north. She loved her job and all the things it stood for, but at times the grating parts were extraordinarily annoying.

The lone female in a family with three brothers, moving off the ranch and onto the RCMP force had meant a lot in terms of gaining respect. The work was usually emotionally fulfilling. After the hours of training she'd completed to reach this point, she was certain this was where she was supposed to be, high school liaison assignments notwithstanding.

But today time dragged, the only high point to look forward to the moment she could put her phone on speaker and call Mitch. Between crap assignments and her crappy partner situation, she needed something to anticipate to give her the strength to last the shift.

HOME FROM work at the garage, showered and scrubbed, Mitch relaxed on his couch and waited eagerly for Anna's call.

Only it wasn't her number that lit the screen.

Damn. He stabbed the phone on. "Go away."

Len's laugh echoed over the line. "Ass. The correct response is 'what can I do for you, master of the universe?'"

"No, the correct response is 'go away, annoying little brother'." Although said *little brother* was the size of a brick shithouse. "I already spent all day with you and the rest of our crazy kin at the shop."

"So here's your chance for some quality time with your favorite brother. I found out there's racing down in Blackstone's fields tonight."

Okay, that caught Mitch's attention. "Really? I thought he'd outlawed their use."

If Len so much as hesitated, Mitch would turn the adventure down. The risk wasn't worth it. Not with him intent on sweet-talking Anna Coleman to the dark side. Getting arrested wouldn't help his cause.

"It's not the same as before," Len insisted. "Gary Blackstone will be there. He's bringing a bunch of friends from out of town, and he invited us specifically. His dad just wants assurances we keep the bikes out of the canola."

"So old man Blackstone won't call the cops when he hears a bunch of motors tearing it up in the distance?"

"Gary says we're good." Len turned on the charm. "You've been dying to try out the rebuild. Come on. You know you want to."

Hmm. A change of plans might actually work to his advantage. "You bringing a date?"

Len laughed. "No. I'm going biking. I hadn't made plans to bring anyone along."

Mitch grinned, flicking on the TV in the background as he considered. His little brother had one woman in his life who was as good as stalking him. "I bet Janey would go with you last-minute."

"Fuck you," Len shot back.

"Just saying. The girl's got your number. Don't know why you're fighting her off so hard."

"Maybe the chase is part of the fun," Len drawled.

Oh hell, yeah. Mitch understood that one and relented on the baiting. Flash-decision time. "I'll meet you at the garage at six thirty, and we'll pick up the bikes."

Anna's call came through right after he'd hung up on Len.

"Tell me you've got something wicked planned," she begged. "I just spent the last hour of my shift rounding up cows with the Laings."

"Come on over, and I'll show you," Mitch teased.

"Deal. Warm up the shower, though, 'cause I stink."

Mitch eyed his watch. He figured that gave him fifteen minutes to get ready before she arrived at his place. He tossed supper together, thankful again he'd found a place deep in the woods to rent. Privacy he had by the bucket-load. It was the only reason he knew Anna would show up.

Secret affair—the cop and the biker. But if he had his way tonight their secret was getting out.

She knocked on the door, and he let her in, only her phone was still glued to her ear and she wore a desperately frustrated expression.

"But why is this the first I'm hearing of it?" Anna demanded. She toed off her shoes and tossed him a quick wave. "No, you didn't tell me. I'm one hundred percent sure... Well, Dad, telling the boys doesn't mean I find out anything. I'll see if I can get the time off, but it's late to ask—"

Mitch moved in, and Anna retreated, mouthing *I smell* as she frantically waved him off.

"—no, I can't just take time off whenever I want. That makes no sense. I have a job, remember?"

Family. So much fun. Mitch stepped aside and gestured down the hall.

"I'll try. Talk to you later." Anna hung up then shoved her phone into a pocket as she stomped away and disappeared into the bathroom.

She was only gone for five minutes. Not nearly long enough for Mitch to linger over mental images of her in the water, hot soapy suds clinging to her strong curves.

Not long enough for her to forget whatever it was that had pissed her off. She wandered back into the living area, yanking a brush through her hair. She'd pulled on a sweatshirt and neat new jeans, and he wanted so badly to mess her up.

Instead he pushed the stewpot toward her.

Anna raised a brow. "You have a strange definition of wicked."

Her skeptical tone made him laugh. "Eat, then we'll talk details."

Another hesitation followed as she examined the meal on the table. *Oh right.* One of her early ground rules—this thing between them was about sex, and nothing else. Well, that rule was about to get crushed and repealed if he had his way.

Mitch tossed her a look. "You're not hungry?"

"Starving, but..."

He nudged the bowl again. "Forget the excuses, stop thinking about what this is, and feed your damn stomach."

She sat hard enough the chair opposite him creaked, but at least now she was smiling. And by the time her bowl was empty, the tension stiffening her shoulders had drained away.

Anna sopped up the last of the thick liquid with her bread. "Mitch Thompson, you make a better stew than I do."

"Man's got to eat. Had enough?"

She nodded, chewing happily as she leaned back.

Mitch slid everything on the table between them to one side. "Ready for some fun?"

The way her gaze bounced off the cleared table space warned him she was thinking far dirtier than he was. At least right now.

When he tossed her a notepad, her face fell.

Mitch snickered. "You were expecting me to lean you over and fuck you for dessert?"

Her eyes flashed. "Are you taking requests?"

"Maybe." Except, now started the next step. "We've been fooling around for months, and I promised to make all your fantasies come true. I need to know what else you want."

"I could just tell you." Anna shook the notepad in the air. "I feel like I'm back in an endless efficiency lecture at work."

A rude noise escaped Mitch. "Stop bullshitting. Just write down the things that come to mind we haven't tried that you'd really like to do."

"With you?"

"Hell, yeah."

"How dirty can I get?"

He grinned.

Anna's smile bloomed. "You win. This is much better than a staff meeting."

No hesitation. Just like she had done since they'd started this *relationship,* Anna dove in. Pen to paper, writing rapidly.

He'd jotted down his items beforehand, which meant he had the time to observe her. Call it cheating if you want, but he'd figured he had to have his plan fully in place to have a chance for it to work, and besides, he loved to watch her move. Even if it was just rocking in her chair while wearing a determined expression.

The moments when her naughty smile broke through were too brilliant to miss.

Her pen paused, and Mitch straightened instantly. "What?"

She wrinkled her nose. "The concept turns me on, but the logistics…"

Now she had his curiosity tweaked. "Put it down anyway, we'll see what we can do."

They both went back to their notepads, but Mitch was ready. Within the next fifteen minutes he'd know if he was going to have his feet kicked out from under him.

As long as he ended up with her on top, he was fine with that.

SHE'D BARELY finished her final sentence when Mitch hauled the pad from under her fingers, exchanging it for his. He flashed his high-beam smile and dropped onto the couch.

Anna shook her head. "So eager to find out my kinks?"

"Of course."

He patted the spot beside him on the soft leather cushion, but Anna ignored him. It was important to maintain a little space until they got to the actual sex.

"Let's just see what turns your crank." She cleared her throat and read the first statement out loud. "Take you dancing at Traders." *What?* Anna glanced at where he sprawled lazily before her. "That's not dirty."

"The way I do it, it is," Mitch leered, his gaze stroking her and making her blood pressure rise. "Plus, I'd expect you to wear those sexy red high heels."

Anna made a face before reading the next item...

...and the next, her anticipation turning to panic faster than she'd have thought possible.

Shit. She was in big trouble. She shot to her feet and dashed to the couch, reaching for the pad Mitch was reading.

"Uh-uh. I'm not done," he warned, holding the pages out of reach.

Anna ignored how rude her actions were. She crawled over him, scrambling to retrieve her list. "You cheated. Give it back."

He wrapped an arm around her, and the next thing she knew she was on the couch under him, wrists trapped in his firm grasp. His dark eyes pinned her in place as well. "I don't cheat."

Her heart raced, half from the position they were in, half from the knowledge of what she'd written on the pad he held from her. "Mitch. You said to list all the things—"

"—we want to try with each other. Right. And that's what I did."

"This is not about—"

He kissed her. Full-on-sexy, brain-melting kiss with lots of tongue and enthusiasm. The out-of-the-blue attack interrupted her words, to start with, then totally messed with her train of thought until she could barely remember what she wanted to complain about in the first place.

When he finally let her up for air, happy endorphins were buzzing through her veins harder than the frustration grating her nerves. "I didn't write that I wanted to be kissed senseless," she protested out of principle.

"I'll add it to my list."

She sighed heavily, the weight of him on top of her making it tough to stick to her guns. "This isn't supposed to be about dating."

Mitch shrugged. "It didn't start that way, no. But I think our plans should change."

"Mitch." Her tone was somewhere between exasperated and tormented.

He set her free, pulling her to her feet and against his body. "Go on, admit it. You like me."

"Of course I do," Anna snapped. "That has nothing to do with whether I'll officially date you or not."

His brows went up, and she had to admit her comment sounded damn stupid. Stupid or worse, rude, as if he was good enough to fuck but not good enough to date, and that was another rabbit hole entirely she'd been ignoring for months.

Mitch skimmed his fingers over her neck then sank them into her hair. "Do you trust me?" he asked, tugging lightly to lift her face toward him.

There was no other answer she could give. "I wouldn't have started this if I didn't."

That gorgeous square-cut jaw with the heavy stubble moved closer, until he was brushing her cheek with his. Every word became a sensual tease. "Give it a try, Constable. Walk on the wild side with me. We'll go as slow as you feel comfortable, but you know I'm not the big bad wolf everyone makes me out to be."

"You still have enormous teeth," she teased, involuntarily trying to shift away as he nibbled on her neck. "Mitch. How could this possibly work between us? I'm a cop."

"And I'm a decent, upright citizen living in your community," he insisted. "Who drives a little fast at times."

She shivered under his touch. The temptation was there, honesty made her admit that. For all his tattoos and fast bike and beefed-up truck—Mitch had never been proven connected with anything more scandalous than a speeding ticket.

Tickets *she'd* given him while he'd flirted unmercifully until she agreed to meet with him.

And now? Was she really going to get involved even more? What would her family say? What would—

Her job.

Fear rose like a barricade, and she tangled her fingers in his hair, tugging him away to stop him from tormenting her body. "I don't want to do anything to risk my position, Mitch. That's all on me—on the expectations the organization has for their officers."

"Not going to mess with your career, babe. I swear."

Anna leaned her head on his chest and fought to draw strength from him. She let out an aggravated growl. "How can I want to say yes so badly, yet want to run out the door at the same time?"

He held her close, strong fingers rubbing over her back. "Tell me what you want, and I'll do what I can to make it happen," he promised. "Take a chance, Anna. Take a step into the unknown and see how it feels."

She glanced at his list. The page lay face-up on the coffee table by their legs. Dancing at Traders. A movie at the theater. A starlight walk. Some of the things he'd written down weren't too frightening to imagine. "You'll go at my speed?"

He laughed softly. "You're as heavy on the gas as I am. I promise to go slower than your speed if we have to."

Temptation hung before her. All she had to do was reach out and take it. "What are we going to do? One item off your list, one item off mine? Mine are a hell of a lot..."

"Filthier than mine? Oh, babe, I noticed." Mitch lifted her chin. "I'm looking forward to making every one of them come true."

Anna hesitated then gave in and took what she wanted. "Okay. We can try it, see how things work. What's the first thing on your list, then? And remember you promised me crazy excitement."

His dark eyes snapped with enthusiasm as a satisfied smile stretched across his face. "Tonight? We're going dirt biking."

Chapter Three

STUPID TO be having butterflies, but they were there as she followed Mitch's bike to the family garage just off Main Street.

He'd offered her a ride from his house, but Anna felt the need to maintain more control. If she had her own vehicle at least she could leave when she wanted to. If things got awkward. If she panicked...

Oh God, what was she *doing*? Had she really agreed to go out with Mitch? So many things could go wrong. So many things were waiting to turn and bite her on the ass on this one.

Only by the time they pulled into the large service area behind the Thompson and Sons shop, a strange sort of peace had settled in.

Either that, or she'd gone numb.

Cars in queue to be repaired were lined up in neat rows, and she pulled into an open space between two of them. She waited until Mitch parked before joining him beside a truck hitched to a low, flatbed trailer filled with a half-dozen bikes.

One of Mitch's younger brothers was there. Len eyed her cautiously, but didn't say anything as he tightened security straps holding the bikes in place.

Mitch swatted Len with his helmet. "Don't be a rude ass. You forget how to say hello?"

"Just threw me for a minute there, bro. I figured you were getting arrested for sure this time if she'd followed you home." Len's face twisted into a smile, one nearly as devastating as Mitch's. He held out a hand to Anna. "Good to see you."

"Len." She ignored the question in his eyes and moved forward after shaking his hand, checking out the load he was tying down. "Nice assortment of bikes."

"We've been working on them off and on all summer. This one Mitch built entirely from salvaged pieces." Len patted the seat of a sleek silver monster.

"And tonight she's getting dirty." Mitch had moved into position opposite her, a full trailer separating them. But as he spoke he looked straight into her eyes, and a delicious shiver eased over her skin.

He wasn't talking about the damn bikes, and they both knew it.

"You guys have an extra helmet I can borrow?" She dragged her gaze off Mitch, checking out the load as she casually sauntered around to his side. If she'd committed to going this far, she had to take that next step.

Besides, she figured Mitch knew ways to keep Len from gossiping.

"Len, grab Anna a helmet," Mitch ordered. "Got everything else loaded?"

"In the back of the truck. Anna—you want a face shield or not?"

"Give her a full," Mitch answered before she could. His grin shone white against his tanned skin as she moved closer. Len was on his way back to the shop, and Anna took her boldness one step farther than even she expected. She eased into full contact with Mitch.

The entire front of their bodies connected as she stared up at him. "Getting me dirty tonight, are you?"

His hand wrapped around her hip. A solid, controlling weight that made interesting flutters start in her belly. "Going to let you fly a little before anything else, though."

He used the hand on her body to twist her with him and bring her to the driver's door. Anna crawled in and sat in the middle of the bench seat, the fresh scent of gas and oil sharp enough to make her wrinkle her nose. Mitch settled beside her, rolling down his window before draping an arm around her shoulders and snuggling her in tight.

There would be no mistaking their positioning for anything other than a relationship of some sort. She wasn't just a casual passenger sharing a ride to the tracks. The heat radiating between them soothed and excited her, and Anna threw the final tethers of caution to the wind. If she was going to do this thing, she was going to have to take chances. She'd have to trust.

A weight lifted off her. Whatever happened, it was worth taking the risk.

Mitch stroked the back of her neck with his strong fingers. "That was a big sigh," he noted. "You think of other things you'd rather be doing?"

"Hell, no. No more sighing," she promised, watching Len make his way across the yard with helmets in either hand. "I'm scared to death in a way, but I plan to enjoy myself even while my head is telling me I'm insane."

Mitch inched closer. "There's crazy and there's *crazy*, and trust me, you're the good type. Relax. Have some fun. Use that need for speed you keep tucked away."

Len pulled the passenger door open and Mitch eased back slightly. His brother's questioning glances were mixed with a cocky grin, and it was all Anna could do to not snipe at him to tell him to stop it.

They traveled down the road for a bit, easy conversation about nothing flowing between them.

"Oh, hey. I phoned Gary to let him know we'd be there." Len tapped his fingers on the dash in time with the music he'd turned on. "He said to park on the north side of the field."

"Got it." Mitch leaned forward. "For the record, you gloat any louder, and I'll knock you into tomorrow."

Len attempted to wipe his grin off, his gaze taking in both Anna and Mitch. "Gloat? Me? I'm the soul of discretion. Although I will say it's about time."

They pulled into the field, fresh air pouring in the window and igniting Anna with a kind of eagerness she hadn't felt for a long time. As if she were struggling her way out of a cocoon, getting ready to spread her wings.

"Len, let's set up Old Charlie for Anna to try first. I'll take the ATK."

"Good idea." Len tapped Anna's arm. "You know how to ride?"

That slow sense of coming alive unfurled in her chest, but she held back from grinning too hard. "A little."

31

Mitch snorted. "Len, use your brains. Anna grew up with Steve and Trevor out on Coleman land. You think she's never ridden before?"

"Didn't want to assume," Len apologized.

Then she was being pulled out Mitch's door, her feet hitting the hard packed dirt on either side of his boots. Anna looked around, eager to get started, but Mitch didn't let her go.

She looked up into a far more serious expression than expected. "What?"

Mitch stroked a thumb over her cheek, his touch lingering and affectionate. "Thank you for coming out tonight. Thank you for agreeing to try this with me. You're one hell of a woman."

All her fears seemed irrational in light of the passion in his eyes. She rubbed her cheek against his hand for a second. It was time for them to go public? They might as well do it right. "One hell of a woman who plans to ride you hard tonight."

The double entendre shot all seriousness away like she'd hoped, and suddenly her cocky, arrogant hoodlum was back in control. "You wish, babe. You wish."

A half-dozen guys were hauling bikes out of the backs of trucks and off trailers, and the area turned into a hotbed of activity. Anna helped where she could, her thick gloves and sturdy leather jacket protecting her from the cooling night air. They were a good group, and she laughed as they teased and prepped their rides. One by one they hit the track, engines revving at an ear-splitting level before they took off, dirt spinning from under their rear wheels.

She was getting ready to straddle the big bike Mitch had loaned her when Gary Blackstone wandered over, his concern and puzzlement clear. "We have permission to use this area."

Anna glanced over her shoulder to see who he was talking to when it hit. "Oh, no—don't worry. I'm not here as a cop. Mitch invited me to ride."

Gary's eyes widened. "Well. Cool."

"All your friends look eager," Mitch noted as he slid in behind Anna.

"They're already taking bets on who will crash first." Gary couldn't take his eyes off her and Mitch, especially when Mitch settled a hand around her waist.

The move might have seemed casual, but Anna knew better. Mitch was staking a very public claim. She screwed up every ounce of *what the fuck* she had and let herself lean against his hard, muscular body.

This time Gary grinned. "Look forward to seeing what you can do out there, Anna. Maybe you'd like to put some bets on the line as well."

"You trying to get out of paying those parking tickets?" she teased.

Mitch chuckled and pulled her with him. "Enough chatter. Time to ride."

SHE WAS glorious when she let loose. Was there any wonder why he'd fallen so hard?

Mitch paused on the top of the rise and pulled off his helmet to better take in the action. Engines whined around him, roars reverberating off the coulee walls. The occasional backfire echoed like a shotgun blast, but all the riders were safe and riding hell-bent for leather.

A typical fall night. Enthusiasm cranked up to eleven before the snow flew and killed their fun.

They'd turned their trucks to face the track, headlights strategically aimed like spotlights as the sun set and dusk painted the arena with an unworldly red glow.

Anna was right smack dab in the middle of the current battle to be the first around the track.

She'd found her groove on the second bike he'd put her on, the machine more manoeuvrable than the old clunker he'd given her first off. He'd figured it was like letting her get her balance on an old reliable nag before handing her the reins to a wild mustang, but he shouldn't have worried. The lone female in the Moonshine Coleman clan knew how to ride, and he was so damn glad.

In this area the Blackstone land was a mass of dips and twists, unusable for anything, even grazing. Back in the day as teens, they'd snuck out here and set tracks for their mountain bikes. They'd built ramps and jumps with shovels before screaming down the hills for hours of fun before chores called them away.

Grownup boys had bigger toys.

Three bikes rose toward the top of a hill, racing to get there first. Len took off at too hard an angle and burnt out, tires skidding sideways as he lost control.

One of Gary's friends, Dustin, hit straight on and rose skyward, his bike catching air under the rims. He twisted the handlebars a few times for show before dropping toward the earth. Anna was hard on his backside, her lighter weight letting her rise even higher, propelled upward by the steep angle and her scorching-fast speed. Mitch sucked for air as she clung to the bars, but let her legs free from around the bike, shooting them out behind her to pause in a layout position.

A second later she'd hauled herself back onto the seat, but the touch of showboating had Mitch's heart racing, a shout of delight torn from his lips to join the other riders' hoots rising skyward.

Had he thought she was amazing? She was more than that, but he was also going to smack her ass for giving him a heart attack.

Which was not a bad thing to look forward to, all things considered. Imagining the sweet curves of her naked butt all rosy and heated under his palm made his groin tighten with anticipation.

The dim red light Mitch had seen in the trees grew stronger, mixed with flashing blue, and everyone in the field pulled to a stop as a police truck bounced its way along the rough access road. The headlights rocked like a drunken lightening bug steadily crawling forward.

Ah, fuck, what now?

Mitch pulled his helmet back on and rolled down the hill to where Gary was getting off his bike. They left their helmets behind and stepped forward to face the approaching cruiser.

"It was fun while it lasted." Len strode from the shadows and joined them.

"Don't worry," Gary insisted. "There won't be any trouble."

Mitch folded his arms across his chest as the last person he wanted to see stepped from the RCMP driver's side, pausing to adjust his hat. Anna's sometime-partner Nick glanced around the strangely lit field, another constable emerging from the passenger side. "No, but it could get interesting," Mitch muttered.

He wasn't sure how Anna was going to react to this twist, but one thing was for certain, there was no keeping their decision to get involved a secret. Not with Nick the Nose pacing forward.

The man was a complete enigma to Mitch. Seemed nice enough, in a fake, squeaky-clean-yet-greasy kind of way. He showed up in the strangest places, at the strangest times, usually to give Mitch grief. Nick had an agenda, but damn if Mitch could figure it out.

The RCMP moved forward, a wide, insincere smile on his face. "You boys having a good time?"

Boys. *Fuck that.* Nick was maybe five years older than the group gathered.

"We were. You want to turn off the flashing lights?" Gary asked. "Makes the place look like a crime scene, and I don't want Gramma Martin to get curious enough to come exploring through the fields on her ATV. She leaves gates open, and next thing we'll be rounding up cattle in the dark."

Nick ignored the request as he glanced over the group of bikes drawing nearer. "If you all have your registration and insurance, I'd appreciate you getting them out."

"For real?" Len moaned.

"You can't be serious," Gary protested. "This is private property—"

"—and no one drove here or plans to leave from this location by crossing crown land?" Nick demanded.

"Nope. Every one of the bikes was transported as required by law." Mitch gestured to the trailers, delighting in Nick's visible dismay. The man wasn't so cocky now that he'd discovered there was nothing illegal or immoral going on.

Nick tried again. "All off-road vehicles need to have front and rear lights—"

"They do." Mitch cut him off. "Tough to see where you're going in the dark without them."

Mitch didn't look away as Nick stared him down, tension rising. Yes, he'd been rude. No ruder than Nick, though.

Gary interrupted before Nick could speak again. "Look, this is my family land, and I cleared the group with my father. Did someone complain? Because there really shouldn't be an issue."

Nick shook his head, gesturing the other RCMP forward. "No complaints, just heard you were going to be here and thought it was a good chance to check..."

The rest of his words were drowned out as the final bike roared up to the gathering. Mitch fought to keep his approval from showing.

Anna skidded to a stop less than five feet from where Nick stood. She cut the engine, and in the contrasting silence someone snickered. The sound prodded Nick to straighten, becoming all official and looming.

"That bike is too large for you. I need some identification and proof of age," he snapped at Anna. He spun toward the rest of the group. "Who's responsible for this rider? All operators under fourteen must have an appropriately sized vehicle and be under the direct supervision of an adult."

The situation was too tempting. Mitch shifted forward. "Well, hell, I volunteer to supervise her, but I'm pretty sure she's over fourteen."

Anna was off the bike and crossing the narrow gap toward her coworker, peeling off her helmet to reveal her long, brown hair.

"Anna?" Nick gasped.

"Nick." She propped the helmet on her hip. "You trying to track me down?"

He shook his head, shock still painting his features.

She leaned around him and waved at the other RCMP. "Stewart. You guys are working late."

Stewart finally spoke. "I'm on patrol tonight. Nick offered to join me."

Anna glanced around at the group. "Any reason to keep them off their bikes? Most of these guys came from out of town, and I think they'd like to get in some more riding."

Stewart cleared his throat. "No problems." His smile was far more sincere than Nick's as he turned to the riders. "You're all good. Thanks for following the safety rules and have a great time tonight."

He basically hauled Nick to the cruiser. The red and blue flashing lights clicked off as the truck edged back, then turned around in the high grass.

The gathered riders slowly scattered, Gary's friends muttering amongst themselves. Anna stood in the spotlight of the retreating RCMP taillights, mud spattered over her jeans and jacket, and an unreadable expression on her face.

Mitch wanted to jump her right then and there, but he waited, torn between hope and fear.

Last thing he'd expected to happen—how was she going to take having Nick of all people show up the first time they went out in public?

The RCMP truck was just disappearing into the trees when Anna let out a shout nearly as loud as the roar of dirt-bike engines once again filling the night air. She faced Mitch with devil-may-care delight pouring from her in waves. "Well, then, I guess there's no turning back now."

Thank God. He stepped to her side and nudged her helmet. "I know a good way to work off some steam."

Heat flashed in her eyes a second before she gave him a wink. "So you keep saying. I think I'm going to need some proof of that."

Hell, yeah. Mitch calculated how soon they could get rid of Len and the bikes, and get back to his place.

Chapter Four

THE MATRESS bounced under her, and Anna laughed, scrambling to recover quicker than Mitch could throw himself after her.

Too late. He caught her by the thigh and dragged her back, flipping her over and pinning her to the bed with his full strength. He hovered above her, his hands trapping her wrists on either side of her head. "God, woman, I want to do everything with you. Trying to decide what to do first is like delicious torture."

"I gave you a list—*oh*..." Anna arched her back and rubbed her chest against him as he lightly bit her neck. "That's nice. You can keep doing that."

His lips were soft on her skin, his breath teasing her cheek. "Your list is perfect, and dirty, but I need to add a few things. Things I think you'd have put on there if you'd thought of them."

"Hmm, okay." As long as he kept touching her she wasn't going to complain. She turned her lips toward him as he licked a path to her mouth. "If I don't like it, I'll tell you."

Their mouths in contact, breaths mingling as he spoke. "You'll like it."

A lazy, thorough kiss followed that had her relaxing back onto his bed. Mitch stretched her hands over her head, locking his fingers around both her wrists as he pressed their torsos together even tighter. With his free hand he teased a trail down her arm, lingering over her breast before tugging her shirt free from her pants. Cool fingers stroked up and over her waist until he cupped a breast in his palm.

The kiss continued, slow and seemingly casual except for how much attention he gave to her every reaction. Easing off at the right moment, pressing for more the next. Even with their lips connected, he got her shirt unbuttoned, her bra loosened off. His thumb teased out a wicked response as her nipple beaded tight under his expert touch.

Contentment rolled through as he released her, pulling her shirt and bra free and tossing them to the floor.

"Well, that was a great appetizer. What's the main course?" Anna stroked the front of his shirt, circling her fingertips over the small buttons. Naked from the waist up, yet at complete ease with him.

Mitch put his hands to his belt, grin widening. "First, I need this."

Oh *God.* "I need that too," Anna teased, eyeing the bulge in the front of his jeans. "Hmm, where's the beef?"

He laughed. "You don't get my cock yet, greedy woman, although I'm looking forward to seeing your lips wrapped around me before the night is over. Right now I need my belt."

Belt? "Oh, I don't know about—"

"Uh-uh," he warned. Mitch pulled the leather free even as Anna curled upward. "Don't assume. If you don't like the things I do you tell me to stop, but wait and see before you make a judgment call. Now lie down."

She eased back on the bed, obeying him but not certain this was a great idea. "Mitch…"

He wrapped the belt around her wrists, leaning over to once again extend her arms over her head. This time when he let go she remained trapped, the strong leather firmly attached to the headboard. Laid out like an erotic banquet before him as he took a slow, ravenous examination of every single inch.

An involuntary shiver rippled over her skin, hard enough to rock the bed.

He pressed his lips to her cheek briefly. "See? You're enjoying this. Ready for the next thing?"

Her mouth had gone dry, and licking her lips did nothing to ease the tension. Her heart rate had doubled, maybe tripled, just from watching his expression. The hunger in his eyes was so intense, so focused as he kept his gaze fixed on her at all times.

She gave up on talking and nodded.

He undid the button on her waistband, his knuckles brushing against her stomach. She sucked in a quick gasp, a beat of desire pulsing deep inside as he pulled down her zipper and tugged the pants over her hips.

"God, you and your sexy underwear." Mitch shook his head, nostrils flaring as he took a deep, satisfied breath. "Every time I see you in your uniform I picture this—see-through fabric, deep red against your skin.

Lace and frills under your starched and stiff formal outfit."

"Undressing me in your head, are you?"

He leaned over her until there was no way she could miss the heated expression on his face. "Every. Damn. Time."

Anna helped, lifting her hips as he pulled her panties free, and then she was bare before him. Completely naked, tied in place, and wondering what came next.

He stripped down and joined her, her gaze greedily taking in the feast of manhood on display while he remained standing. The tats on his arms created full sleeves of fiery crimson and deep orange. Flames licked from shoulders to wrists, nearly as hot as the man himself. The fire pattern continued over his back and chest, morphing into chain links draped over his torso that came alive between the ink shading and his flexing muscles.

She never questioned him about the design before, although she'd wondered.

"Why the chains?" she asked as he crawled onto the mattress next to her. The heat from his skin was hot enough to brand her as he tugged their bodies together. "What are you keeping caged?"

Mitch's expression turned thoughtful even as he continued to caress her, slipping his fingers over her hip and cupping her ass. The hard length of his cock was trapped between them, her breasts crushed against his rock-solid chest. Her arms were still stretched over her head, adding a harsher, more dangerous edge to the entire setting.

"I'd never thought of that," Mitch confessed. "Of caging a beast or anything. The chains are a reminder that simple things are important."

That's all he said before his lost-in-thought haze sharpened and he looked her in the eye. His hand drifted lower, off her ass, and he tugged her thigh over his hip.

The position left her wide open and vulnerable, the cooler air swirling around them connecting with the hot moisture of her sex. "You've barely touched me and I'm already dying to have you inside me," she confessed.

He snuck his fingers lower, stroking past the crack of her ass, lingering where she was longing for him to get to work. "You're wet. I like that. Only I bet you're going to be wetter in a minute. Keep your leg over my hip," he ordered.

She waited, tempted to pulse her hips forward to find something to make contact with to ease the growing ache inside.

Mitch lifted his hand away, and she moaned in protest.

Only to gasp a second later as he snapped his hand down and smacked her butt cheek.

"*Jesus*. What the hell?" Anna squirmed, but he had her caught in position. His strong hand gripped her thigh and pinned them together. "Crap, Mitch, that stung."

He laughed. "It's going to sting some more before we're through, babe."

A second strike landed, a little lower, just as hard, and the throbbing that had started inside shot outward and upward into a Mitch-sized-hand area on her ass. "You *shit*. You tied me up so you could spank me?" Anna growled in disbelief.

Mitch rubbed his hand over the stinging portion of her butt. "Don't knock it yet."

She opened her mouth to protest, but he sucked the words from her mouth, kissing her again with the wildness she craved. Distracting her from the fact he'd probably left a print on her skin.

It was too easy to focus on all the other things she was enjoying. The demanding stroke of his tongue, the way he used his entire body when he kissed her, small movements reminding her again and again that they were stark naked and only inches away from being joined.

When he pulled back, his eyes had gone fiery. His dark needs and wild passion clear for her to witness. Maybe the chains he'd tattooed onto his skin were to help him remember something, but her idea of a wild beast being chained and controlled wouldn't have been inappropriate either.

"Trust me?" he asked again.

Anna breathed out slowly, ignored that part inside that screamed she was being a fool, and nodded.

Mitch tugged her leg a little higher over him, and the change of position tilted more of her ass toward the ceiling. More for him to put his hand on when he smacked down.

She tightened up on the first strike, nothing registering but stinging pain and a sense of playing a game she wasn't really into. Mitch spanked her three times in rapid succession then smoothed his palm over the hot surface, small circles, easing the pain and...

...increasing a sensation she hadn't expected.

Pleasure?

45

If it was, it was a new type than she'd experienced before. Something less like the cool slick of satisfaction from biting into a sweet, juicy ripe pear, juices coating her lips. This was more along the lines of having her mouth catch fire from a great bowl of spicy jambalaya.

"There you go," Mitch whispered. "Trust me and enjoy yourself."

He spanked her another dozen times, alternating sides. The palm of his hand connected with her tingling flesh with a sharp crack. Every swat landed in a slightly different spot. There was no way to anticipate where the blow would strike, not trapped up close to him like she was.

By now she honestly didn't care.

"My God, what have you done to me?" There was no keeping quiet as he worked her over. Every blow she moaned or sighed. Every time he paused to caress her heated ass, she gasped to get air into her depleted lungs.

He shifted her slightly again, her thigh resting well up his body. This time when his hand made contact, it was on the lips of her sex.

Anna nearly shot off the bed.

"God damn, you're so fucking beautiful." Mitch caught her chin with one hand, locking her gaze on his. With his other hand he slipped his fingers between her folds and hummed in happy approval. "You're dripping wet. Your pussy is so ready for this."

"You're killing me," Anna got out before the next spank landed, and then she wasn't able to speak anymore.

The world reduced to Mitch's hand and the incredible, unfathomable pleasure he was creating in her body. Every time he connected with her labia streaks of white shot before her eyes, like electric pulses that had begun far lower expanding in an uncontrollable web through her entire body. Usually before an orgasm the tension started deep inside, but this time it was her clit and the lips of her labia that tingled and tightened. Hot and getting hotter.

Another slap, and another. The moisture from her pussy changed the sound of the strikes from crisp snaps heard during the earlier smacks to her ass. Wetter. Strange yet erotic, and combined with Mitch's dirty whispering, she teetered on the edge of something immense.

"Your ass is glowing red, Anna. Hot and dirty, and so fucking gorgeous. I can see where my hand has been, like I've branded you, just for tonight. You like it when I spank your pussy, don't you? Rocking into me every time, wanting more." Another set of strikes landed, Anna's moan mixed with the echoes. "Juicy and hot—ready for my cock. Or for my tongue if I decided to lick you first until you scream."

"Your cock," Anna begged. "*Please*, fuck me. Fuck me now."

Only a second later Mitch slipped out from under her. He rolled her to her belly, dragging her down the bed. Her arms were fully extended overhead, her face to the mattress, her legs spread as he pushed his knees between hers. Mitch caught her hips and raised them slightly, his groin briefly coming in contact with her still-throbbing ass.

He lined up his cock and thrust.

Anna arched back her neck and screamed. "*Mitch.*"

All the nerves he'd primed earlier blazed. He plunged in, slapping their hips together as he drove deep.

His cock spread her, his piercing rubbing against the tender walls of her passage. The new position meant that he covered her, his naked chest to her back, head tucked beside hers. He jerked his knees to the outside of her legs and pressed her limbs together. The position changed the angle of his thrusts, reducing how far he could pump, but increasing her sensation of being *taken*.

Tied to the bed, his body a heavy weight over hers as he fucked her relentlessly, Anna's excitement transformed. She was completely aware of every move he made, and yet a happy haze blurred their surroundings. Unperturbed fascination set in with what Mitch was doing to her.

Using her for his own pleasure, if the moans and grunts rumbling from his lips were any indication. Dragging her right along with him, if the noises she couldn't stop from escaping were another clue.

She closed her eyes and pictured what they would look like to someone stumbling into the room. They'd find a wild man ravishing his willing captive. Rough and dirty, and oh my *God,* so good.

Her orgasm struck like a collapsing wall. Between one second and the next her body went from primed to pulsing. Mitch swore and froze, sealed to her from top to bottom with his cock buried deep.

Her pussy squeezed around the thick length, satisfaction pulling free another series of moans. Mitch rocked lightly, pushing the hard metal of his piercing back and forth enough to keep aftershocks twitching her entire body.

When he finally rolled off her, twisting her to the side as he went, Anna barely had the strength to form a smile. "You've fucked me senseless," she gasped out one word at a time.

He released her wrists, pulling her over him and petting her. Rubbing lightly, kissing her face. Taking her down slowly from the extreme high he'd propelled them to.

First night of their changed relationship, and the evening had been spectacular in so many ways. She still had a ton of unanswered questions, especially regarding how the rest of her work team would take the news she was officially dating Mitch.

Yet whatever direction this ride she'd agreed to take with him went, one thing was for certain.

It wasn't going to be boring.

Chapter Five

ONE WEEK later and she'd been too busy to even complain about how busy life had become. There'd been a rash of kids pulling crazy stunts, and sure enough she'd ended up scheduled to work the entire Thanksgiving weekend.

If she wasn't buried in the RCMP office, she'd been run off her feet responding to call-outs while the staff rotated through strange shifts because of the holiday. Monday of the October long weekend rolled around, and she'd basically missed breakfast and lunch trying to keep up with one disaster after another at work.

"Anna, you've got a visitor," the front-desk clerk called.

"One sec, Claire," Anna shouted back. She saved her final notes on the break-ins she and Nick had attended, then grabbed her work jacket, tugging it on as she headed to the entrance.

There had to be a lull at some point.

She approached the secure area that separated casual visitors to the station from the staff. Claire gave her a strange look but moved aside, obviously wanting to ask some questions, but resisting temptation.

A moment later the reason became plain as Mitch's dark brown eyes met Anna's. He was dressed from top to bottom in black. The perfectly cut jeans hugging his legs looked a lot fancier than usual, his leather jacket pulled over a heavy knit sweater that made her fingers itch to see if it was really as soft as it looked. The thick layer of scruff on his chin produced chills as memories of him rubbing the rough texture against her tender skin leapt to mind.

And the grin? Dangerous and addictive.

Anna wanted to sweep open the door and jump him, but she had to keep things somewhat professional. "Mitch. What can I do for you?"

He raised a brow, eyeing the glass and metal separating them. "I was in the area and thought I'd stop by. You nearly done for the day?"

Anna checked her watch. "Half an hour, and I'm off."

Mitch nodded. "I know you missed your family gathering, so can I take you to the café for a late supper? They've got turkey with all the fixings on the menu tonight."

"Cranberry sauce as well?"

"You know it."

His invitation shouldn't have pleased her so much, but she was willing to admit, at least to herself, that it did. "I'd like that."

Another cocky grin. "You want me to wait for you or meet you there?"

Anna considered. "You have your bike or your truck?"

"Truck."

She leaned closer to the glass. "How about this? Go get your bike, and a helmet for me, and you can pick me up at my place. It's a nice night. After we eat you can take me for a ride."

His gaze locked on her lips, his voice dropping to a bare whisper. "I'd never turn down the offer to *take you for a ride*."

A decadent thrill shot through her at his suggestive comment.

Lovely.

Mitch stepped backward, his gaze still fixed on her face. "I'll see you there, then. Do you need a jacket as well?"

"No, I'll get changed at my place."

He winked, then pushed through the exit door, the security buzzer announcing his departure. Anna stared until the door closed and the dark shading on the glass obscured the view of his very fine ass walking away.

She ignored the unasked question in Claire's eyes and made her way back to her office to finish up the final paperwork.

Nick was waiting for her, deep concern on his face as he examined the file she'd left on her desk.

"What's up? Did I miss something on the Cranston case?" she asked.

He put down the papers he'd been poking through, instead pacing across the room. "I didn't say anything the other day, but I have to ask. What's up with you and Mitch Thompson?"

Oh boy. And so it began.

Anna sat, waking her computer and checking the last thing she'd had open. The fact Nick hadn't mentioned finding her at the dirt track had been wonderful—and strange.

She should have known it was too good to last. "Not sure what you're asking."

Nick sighed heavily, his dark eyes focusing sharply on her as he seemed to change the topic again. "It was a shock to discover you in the middle of a bunch of off-roaders. I had no idea you were into that kind of thing."

She shrugged. "Good clean fun, if you don't mind the mud. They're not illegal, and from what I can tell, the Blackstones have gone out of their way to make sure they're not disturbing any of their neighbours."

"Still surprised me," Nick insisted. "With the rise in biker-gang activity all over the province, you might want to rethink being involved in that kind of situation again."

A snort of disbelief escaped before she could stop it. "You're not serious. We were riding dirt bikes, not hogs, and there's no connection whatsoever between any gang activity and those guys innocently tearing up some spare land at the Blackstone property."

"And Mitch?"

Anna rose to her feet and steeled her spine. "Again, not sure what you're asking. Or if it's any business of yours what I do outside of work time."

Nick raised his hands and backed off. "Hey, no need to get snooty. Just—"

"Snooty?" Anna laughed, but there was a touch of anger under her amusement. "Good grief, Nick. Don't try that on me. You have something to say, say it. Don't go suggesting I just dropped a load of teenage angst on you."

"Fine. Straight out, unless you're doing court-ordered community work with him, I would suggest you not be seen in public with Mitch Thompson."

A strange sensation churned her gut—annoyance on Mitch's behalf, and a huge load of disgust at herself for hesitating in getting involved with him earlier. Having Nick toss his unwarranted bias against Mitch in her face only made it that much clearer how wrong she'd been in trying to hide her interest.

She crossed her arms and stared Nick down for a moment before she dared to speak. "Give me one solid piece of evidence you have that puts Mitch on any kind of watch list," she demanded.

Nick opened his mouth then closed it just as quickly. He looked away, refusing to meet her eyes. "He's got all the classic profiling for trouble. That's all I'm saying."

"And I'm saying we judge people by their actions, not the clothes on their back or the marks on their skin." Anna breathed out slowly, fighting for control. "The Thompson family has been in the community for generations. Never a lick of trouble from them."

"He's bad news," Nick insisted.

"Because he's got tattoos? Because he rides a bike, or what? What are you basing your accusations on?"

"The tip sheets clearly—"

"God, Nick, where the hell are you getting these tip sheets you're obsessing over? Because as far as I know tattoos and bikes alone don't push anyone into becoming one of the criminal element."

"Fine," Nick cut in. "You obviously don't want to listen to reason. I'll be around if you need anything, otherwise I won't bring it up again."

He stormed from their office as if he were the injured party. Anna unclenched her fingers that had instinctively curled into tight fists during their *discussion*.

Yet another blot on her conscience that she'd ever given even a moment's thought to Mitch's reputation. She'd been as bad as Nick.

No more.

She headed home, showered and changed quickly in an attempt to scrub off her frustration. It was better to look forward, she decided, and she pulled out all the stops. Fancy silk underwear followed by dabbing perfume on the intimate spots she was sure Mitch would appreciate before the night was over.

In contrast to Mitch's dark outfit, she went for light. A pair of faded stonewashed jeans so old they were buttery soft against her skin. A sturdy, lined leather jacket covered a pale blue turtleneck sweater that clung to her curves like a second skin. High riding boots hugged her calves, and the appreciation in Mitch's eyes when she opened the door made it all worthwhile.

"Holy hell." He examined her another time top to bottom, lingering on certain spots long enough to make her tingle. "Holy *fucking* hell."

"You owe me dinner," she pointed out. "No ravishing me before you feed me."

Mitch tilted his head up and leered that much harder. "You reading my mind, are you?"

"Pretty much figured that's what your expression meant," Anna teased. "Let's get rolling. I'm starved."

She locked the door then accepted the hand he offered, pressing against him eagerly as he curled a hand around her neck and brought their lips together. Heat blazed between them like always, and like always Anna melted a little more.

He pulled back slowly, as if reluctant to relinquish her lips. "We'd better go before they run out of cranberry sauce."

"That would be a travesty," she agreed.

She crawled on the bike behind him, settling her thighs tight to his. Wrapped her arms around his waist and leaned in close. A strong, masculine scent filled her nostrils as she rested her cheek against his back.

There was something so incredible about moving together on the bike. A trust that had to be there, a confidence in Mitch's abilities. A confidence that was clearly well deserved. He handled the bike with ease as they raced down the back streets of Rocky, the heat of his body warming her thoroughly.

He parked on the street a ways down from the café, holding the bike steady until she'd made it to the sidewalk. Anna lingered close, twisting in his arms to smile up into his gorgeous face.

"I can smell the turkey from here." Mitch hummed happily. "Come on."

He linked his fingers through hers and tugged her forward as they wandered the street, glancing in windows. Mitch pointed out the crazy Thanksgiving decorations the local shops had done in the front displays, and Anna laughed at his wry comments.

She was facing the café when a family wandered out. They had only taken a few paces down the sidewalk before the father jerked to a stop. He caught his wife's hand, they both grabbed their kids, and dashed across the street, barely checking first to see if the traffic was clear.

Anna let Mitch guide her. She was too busy examining the mysterious response, especially when the family walked not even half a block before crossing back to get in their van.

Really? She glanced at Mitch, but all she saw was the man who turned her inside out with longing. Who shook her world and wanted to take her for a walk in the moonlight.

Not someone who it was prudent to cross the street to avoid.

They were seated. Menus brought. The entire time Anna was hyper aware of the customers in the café—of them judging, assessing. Finding Mitch wanting, or showing they were afraid of him in some way.

People eyed his arms as he took off his coat and hung it from the hook by their table, pushing up the sleeves of his sweater. Whispers sounded, conversations buzzed, low and interrupted.

Anna wanted to shout at them all to mind their own business.

She'd never been so aware of social bias in her life. Never so ashamed for not fighting it harder. She ignored the questioning looks being cast her direction and deliberately caught his fingers in her own in clear sight of anyone walking past their table.

Mitch rubbed his thumb over her knuckles, his smile softening. "You got something on your mind?" he asked.

She shook her head. "Just happy to be with you."

It was the honest truth. And she was glad.

ANNA WAS like a new person. One with so much fire he could barely control the flames.

He liked it. He liked it a lot.

They'd left the restaurant and headed back to his bike when she pulled him aside. "Wait. I want dessert."

He squeezed her fingers. "You already had one piece of pie. You want to go back for more?"

She shook her head, stepping onto the stairs leading up to the bakery until their heads were on the same level. "Come here," she ordered.

Her firm grip guided him forward until their lips met.

Mitch planned on letting her keep in control since she seemed to have something in mind, but the instant their lips connected the red-hot need blasting through his veins took over. Wiped out all his good intentions. She thrust her fingers into his hair and held him close, but he already had an arm wrapped around her back, fingers splayed wide to give him maximum leverage to lock their torsos together.

She kissed him greedily, undulating against him in an exquisite tease that fired his senses. His cock was hard and getting harder every second. Warning signals went off in his brain, but not loudly enough to make him stop. Her kiss was making his head spin, it was so damn good.

Much longer and he'd be tempted to forget where they were. He'd have his hand shoved up under her baby-soft sweater so he could grope her in full-out public. Mitch pulled himself together and dragged them apart, breathing heavily as he examined her face.

"You're a pistol tonight. Not that I'm complaining, but you have plans?"

"Just making a point to myself," Anna stated. "You and me—we're going out."

Mitch laughed loudly. "Hell, yeah, we are."

Whatever it was that had flipped her switch, he had every intention of enjoying it.

She caught him by the front of his jacket, bold attitude and strength apparent in her every move. "Take me riding?"

He scooped her up, spinning her in a circle before he deposited her on the sidewalk again and led her back to his bike. "I thought we'd head to the mountains."

Her grin widened. "Sounds awesome."

They pulled on gloves and helmets before mounting, then Anna curled around him as if she were his own personal thermal blanket. Mitch debated tossing the extended ride out the window, because with her mood he could hardly wait to see what she'd be like in bed.

Being patient sucked, but then anticipation had a place as well.

For the next hour, the miles slipped past. Cold crisp air around them, the heat of her body like a miniature generator behind his back. There was barely any traffic on this stretch of highway—too late on the holiday weekend for anyone to be heading into the mountains on the lesser-traveled route.

He stopped at the better lookouts so they could take in the mountain views and growing twilight. Also so they could haul off their helmets and neck for a while before the cold forced them back onto the bike.

Mitch stared into the distance as the final curve of the sun disappeared behind the western ridge. Sunset glow lingered, reflecting off the clouds, but the bright light was gone for another day.

Things changed so quickly. For good. For bad.

A warm gentle touch connected with his cheek as she turned his head until he was staring into her pale blue eyes. "You've gone far away," Anna said softly.

"Worried about my sister," he admitted.

"Ahhh." She cupped his face. "Any change since the accident?"

He shook his head. Katy had slid off the road a couple weeks earlier, and while she hadn't been seriously hurt, she'd gotten a head injury. "Saw her yesterday at the family dinner. She's doing okay, but the doctors still don't know what's up with her memory."

"They'll figure it out," Anna assured him.

Mitch hoped so, only it was another thing that haunted him. "I hate how little control we have at times. One minute she was fine, the next, Katy's lost parts of her past—all vanished in a flash. Made me think of my mom passing away years ago. Seemed like it was only a few days between finding out she was sick and her being gone."

Control. He wanted it. *Needed* it, and yet right there with Anna looking up at him with sorrow in her eyes, it was clear that there were so many things he had no influence over.

Anna kissed him again, softer this time, brushing away some of his frustrations. Bringing him back to the things that were good, and that he could control.

The stars were out by the time he turned down the long driveway leading into the trees and his home.

He parked the bike, hauling off his helmet and loving how she right away stepped back into his personal space. "I didn't ask if you wanted me to take you home."

Anna shook her head, following him inside and hanging up her borrowed helmet. "This is exactly where I wanted to end up. Well, almost exactly."

She caught him by the hand and pulled him into the living room. One more tug brought him to a seated position on the couch where she proceeded to crawl on top of him, knees straddling his thighs, her jacket carelessly abandoned beside them.

Anna caught him by the chin, staring him down. "I've been wanting to do this all night long."

She cupped his face softly.

"You've kissed me plenty tonight," Mitch teased, uncertain where she was going with this.

Her head tilted slightly, eyes sparkling in the faint light. "Not just a kiss. My turn to give to you. All of it, everything you need."

"I don't get any choice in what you do?" Mitch's voice didn't sound right, even to him. There was such tenderness in her touch it was making strange emotions flood his system.

He'd fallen in love with her passion, but this side of her—the slow-moving, gentle kisses she was pressing against his lips, his jaw, his neck—he could take this as well with no complaints.

She leaned against his body, sneaking her fingers into the hair at the back of his neck as she kissed her way to his ear. When she whispered, a shiver rolled over his skin.

"You get a choice. You get to choose to enjoy every minute."

Mitch helped her take off his shirt. She traced her fingers over his tats, the teasing touch followed a moment later by her tongue. His vision went dark when

VIVIAN AREND

she reached his abdomen. He must have helped her, but the actual details were lost as to how he now sat bare-ass naked on the couch, his jeans tangled around his ankles because all he could focus on—

Anna's hot mouth on his cock.

Her tongue twirled around his piercings, the sensation all the more intense in the sensitive area. Wetness coated him, her strong fingers wrapped around the base of his shaft as she slipped between his knees and grinned up at him.

"Hell, babe, you have no idea what you're doing to me," he muttered, stroking her hair off her forehead.

She didn't answer with words. Just leaned forward and put those incredible lips to his cock again. Pushed down and enveloped him with heat and pleasure. And when she pulled back, mouth tight as she sucked, Mitch gave himself over to the hedonism of the act. She wanted to blow his mind?

Game on.

He wrapped her long hair around his fingers, this time not to control her but because he couldn't resist. Her head rose and fell in his lap, and he groaned as the tingling urgency in his balls increased so rapidly he knew he was gonna spill before he'd had a chance to really enjoy himself.

"God, you're killing me."

Anna hummed happily, her fingers slipping down to his balls. She added a twist with her tongue, and between the vibration and the extra pressure, he lost it. Stars formed in front of his eyes as he emptied, semen coating her tongue, spraying over her lips and cheeks as she pulled back. She pumped him as he came, new strands flying out to land on her neck and cleavage, and god *damn* if his cock didn't jerk again at the sight.

Mitch collapsed against the couch, a pleasant buzz wracking his body, but it hadn't been enough. Not nearly enough. He somehow found the energy to lean forward and pull her into his lap. One more move and he'd snatched up his T-shirt so he could wipe her grinning face clean.

"You look awfully pleased with yourself," he noted.

"That was fun." She eased against him, relaxed and soft, which was nice, but if she thought they'd reached the cuddling portion of the evening, she had another think coming.

"That was just the beginning," he warned.

Her eyes widened, and the mischief returned. "You ready for more so soon?"

"I'm always ready for more of you."

She shouted in surprise as he rose, cradling her to his chest. Her protests changed to laughter as he was forced to pigeon-step his way down the hall until he got his jeans kicked off, finally lofting her toward his bed and diving after her.

Hours later Anna smiled up at him, her hair tangled, a sheen of sweat on her skin. Sated and glowing and looking so damn content. He'd done that for her, and the idea pleased him far too much.

She curled against his naked torso, tucking her head under his chin. "Happy Thanksgiving, Mitch," she breathed with a happy sigh.

Happy Thanksgiving, indeed.

Chapter Six

MITCH PULLED into his parking spot behind the family garage, blinking wearily as he made his way through the man-door that led to the main work area of Thompson and Sons. Anna had surprised him by crawling into his bed at five a.m. when she'd finished her shift, and there hadn't been a lot of sleep from that moment to now.

His body was satisfied, but his brain needed a gallon of coffee to lose the fuzz.

"Finally," Clay grumbled. "Nice of you to show up."

"It's like ten after seven. Don't be an ass," Mitch sniped back at his older brother as he grabbed a coverall from the shelf.

"Don't bother getting changed." Clay lofted a set of keys his direction. "We need to clear out a few of the older wrecks from the back lot, and you lost the toss."

Shit. Last thing he wanted to do today was haul a trailer full of cars down the icy winter roads all the way to their parts buyer in Calgary. Anna had the next twenty-four hours off, and he'd hoped to cut out of work early to spend time with her after she woke from her nap. "How can I lose the toss when I wasn't even here?" Mitch gave his youngest brother Troy the evil eye. "You bastard."

"You snooze, you lose," Troy taunted. He ran a hand through his dark hair and grinned wildly. "It was between you and Len, actually, but he got in three minutes before you."

The joys of working with family. "Fine. Is the truck ready?"

Clay shook his head. "Len went to hook up the trailer. Grab the manifest from Katy, and we'll get the last of them loaded."

He winked before turning away, and Mitch lost some of his irritation. It wasn't a big deal—he'd handle the change in plans. His brothers weren't that difficult to work with.

In fact, as he took the steps to the office area two at time, his good mood rapidly returned. He paused at the top of the landing to glance back into the work bay. Clay was ushering Troy out one of the oversized garage doors, the rear of the massive trailer moving into sight outside the building. Len joined them, and all three began pointing animatedly around the snow-filled yard at which cars needed to be loaded. Even from his perch, the good-natured banter between them was audible. The kind of noise and confusion only siblings would put up with.

They'd gone through a lot together, him and his family. After losing their mom when Mitch had barely turned sixteen, they'd dealt with whatever life tossed them together, and he was grateful.

65

The red flames on his wrists and arms were a reminder they didn't all cope the same way, but overall they'd always been there for each other. There was no doubt about that.

He turned toward the office door, stopping in his tracks to watch through the window. His dad was explaining something to Katy who wore an expression of sheer frustration.

It was another thing they'd get through as a family. The only visible sign that remained of his baby sister's accident was that her long hair had been shaved to allow for testing, and only a thin layer had regrown since. The lingering nonvisible results were far worse than her buzz cut.

He entered the office.

"You don't need to do math, Katy. Just put the numbers from the receipt into the boxes, and the program calculates them for you." Keith Thompson squeezed his daughter's shoulder. "I can show you again."

She shook her head and waved him off. "No, you have things to do. I'll figure it out."

Keith turned wearily to the door. "If you're sure."

"Dad, stop it. I'm good. Get out and let me do my job." Only Katy's smile melted far too quickly when their father finally left. She lifted tired eyes to Mitch's. "If you want anything to do with numbers, I'll warn you, I might scream."

"Oh, Katy." Mitch crossed the room and offered a hug.

She squeezed him gratefully for a moment before pushing him away. A quick wipe at her eyes cleared away the couple of tears that had escaped, and she put on a smile again. "Who knew that I'd have to repeat second-grade math at my age?"

"Stop it," Mitch soothed. "Accidents happen. You're doing the best you can, and you're getting better."

She shrugged. "Feels a lot like I'm spinning my wheels." Katy made a face as she rubbed her stomach. "And I think I'm coming down with something, which isn't helping."

Mitch sat on the desk and glanced at the mess of papers scattered over the usually pristine surface. "I'm supposed to get the transport manifest from you so I can do the car drop this morning."

Katy nodded. "It's here somewhere." She scrambled through the mess and pulled out a set of papers. "I did them up last night. All the VINs, the bills of sales." She shoved everything into an oversized envelope. "Oh, wait. There was one more..."

She twirled and dug in a desk drawer. Mitch poured himself a coffee while he waited, filling the largest travel mug in the office. "You need me to pick up anything while I'm in Calgary?" he asked.

Her eyes widened, and this time her smile was real. "Seriously? Would you stop by the craft shop and grab me a package? I ordered it online, but forgot to hit the 'deliver to residence' option. It's sitting at the north Michaels store."

Mitch shoved the envelope she handed him under his arm so he could use his free hand to ruffle what little had grown back of her hair. "No problem. Give me the receipt."

It took her another fifteen minutes to track that down, long enough for him to help load the final vehicles on the transport.

"Try not to get pulled over for speeding," Troy teased.

Mitch resisted mentioning his favourite cop was currently passed out naked in his bed. He hadn't made a big deal yet about the fact he was dating Anna. Len knew, and maybe Clay, but Troy didn't always spot what was going on right under his nose. "I'll ignore that you just tried to give me driving advice. It took you how many attempts to get your learner's, baby bro?"

"Butt out, butthead."

Len snickered. "Be thankful he finally passed when he did. Meant we didn't have to drive him around and watch all his boring football games anymore."

Mitch left them still taunting each other about some past wrongs.

If one of his coping strategies had been to tattoo reminders into his skin, each of his brothers had taken a different path over the years. Troy had gotten lost in sports. Len had gone quiet, vanishing at times in a rather astonishing way for someone of his size.

Clay? Had gone overprotective.

"You got everything?" Clay stuck his head in the passenger door and started going through the glove box. "Registration and insurance are—"

"—in the same place we've always kept them. Stop it. I don't need two fathers."

Clay's frown didn't fade completely. "Sorry. Just worried."

Mitch understood his brother's fears, but no way in hell was he going to take being babied, let alone by someone barely a year older than him. "I'm not going off the road, and no one else is going to get hurt. Relax, you're driving me crazy. I can only imagine how much you're pissing Katy off acting like a mother hen."

"I should have…" Clay backed up and backed down. "Fine. I'll lay off for now. Say hi to Denis for me."

Mitch pulled out of the yard, soothed by the power of the enormous car-hauler under his control. He cranked up the music and hit the highway, settling in for the two-hour drive.

His thoughts wandered from Anna, to his family and back to Anna far too quickly. He was growing more certain what he and Anna had was more than explosive chemistry. They fit.

He would take her showing up at his house this morning as a positive sign she was thinking that way about him as well.

Dirty daydreams about her entertained him the entire trip, and he'd bet money there was a foolish grin pasted on his face as he pulled into the craft-shop parking lot to nab Katy's order. He tossed the box on the passenger seat then drove the final fifteen minutes to the salvage yard they'd worked with for years.

For the first time ever a gate blocked the entrance.

"Bullshit on that." Mitch laid on the horn. If he dropped the load in the next half an hour, he might be able to sneak home and catch Anna still sleeping. He could think of all sorts of interesting ways to wake her up.

He was pleased to see someone pop out immediately from the nearby Quonset. The man hurried over and pulled the gate aside, gesturing for Mitch to drive around the side of the oversized metal building.

Another man appeared, hands waving rapidly as he directed Mitch in pulling his big rig around the tight corner. "Jeez. I liked the old setup better," Mitch muttered.

He rolled down the window to give Denis hell, but a man with an unfamiliar face strode to the driver side.

"The changes make it hell to drop off shit. What was wrong with having the delivery doors in the front?" Mitch leaned out the window to eye the torturous back-up job he was going to have to do to get free.

"Yeah, right." The other guy laughed as if Mitch had told the most hilarious joke. "Drop them in the front yard. Good one."

Mitch didn't bother to hide his lack of amusement. "Where's Denis?"

The guy jerked a thumb toward a small ATCO trailer.

The back of the trailer was already down, the first cars being driven out, hitches in place to drag the dead vehicle carcasses out last. Mitch ignored the sudden buzz of workers swarming the place and carried the envelope Katy had given him into the office.

Conversation cut off completely as he stepped through the door, a half a dozen faces twisted his way. All of them stern and forbidding. He searched the room until he spotted Denis.

"Hey," Denis called, rapidly stepping forward. "Thompson and Sons. Good to see you again."

Mitch didn't waste his breath complaining. Just held out the envelope Katy had prepped. They'd been bringing stock to this yard for years, but his father's standard offer came out reluctantly—Mitch didn't like how this entire situation felt. And it wasn't only that everyone in the office was staring at him as if he were the main event at a circus. "You want us to send an invoice?"

"Cash is fine. Let me—"

An alarm sounded, and the silent crowd vanished, chairs overturned as they shoved past Mitch, or raced out the emergency exit at the back of the trailer.

Denis's face had gone a pasty white. He ignored Mitch and ducked behind his desk, snatching up a sack and frantically shoving papers off his desk into it.

Mitch's bad feeling spiked, and he backed toward the main exit. Screw getting their money—

The metal door behind him burst open, slamming into the wall. The order rang out, loud and clear. "Don't anyone move."

Uniformed police poured into the office. Through the window more bodies were visible sweeping into the yard and up to the open back doors of the Quonset.

Fuck. Mitch froze, thankful his hands were empty and in the open. "I'm just here dropping off a shipment."

One of the officers approached him slowly. "Right. That's a likely story."

This was going from bad to worse. "I work at Thompson and Sons garage in Rocky Mountain House." Mitch spoke softly and as calmly as he could under the circumstance. "That's my truck out there. I was doing a routine parts drop. Can you tell me what's wrong?"

There were two of them beside him now, examining him closely as more men pushed past. A loud shout rang out, and he pivoted in time to see Denis make a break for the backdoor before being tumbled to the ground by his pursuers.

God, this was not going to end well at all.

One of the officers beside him caught hold of his arm, pulling it back. Mitch didn't resist, but a cringe shook him as cool metal loops closed around one wrist, then the other, pinning his arms behind him. "Looks like I drove into something I didn't intend to," Mitch insisted. "On the desk. Transport papers for all the vehicles I brought. Bills of sale—it's all there, I swear."

"Don't move," the older officer in front of him warned, the nametag on his uniform spelling *MACKIE* in bold black letters. "Greyson, check out his story."

"Company name is on the side door of the truck. My name is Mitch Thompson, and I have no idea what's going on." Other than his arms already going numb from the awkward position.

Greyson held up the envelope Denis had abandoned. "This one?"

Mitch nodded.

The police pointed at the truck. "Everything in there belong to you?"

"It should. Papers are in the glove box."

Greyson nodded. "Keep cooperating, and we'll check out your story."

He vanished, leaving Mitch in the company of five officers, a couple of whom were systematically emptying desk drawers.

"Sit," Mackie ordered, pointing at the flimsy plastic reception chairs positioned against the wall.

Mitch sat.

He watched out the window as a large group of officers led a line of cuffed and controlled workers into police cars, the yard filled with neon blue and red flashing lights.

Inside the office, police were now working at computer screens as well as the files. Mitch's stomach was in his shoes as the activity continued. This wasn't something small and innocent he'd stumbled into—not with this many police on the case.

Greyson was striding back already, and Mitch's hopes fell further at the icy expression the man wore.

He stomped through the office entrance and handed the envelope back to Mackie. "Numbers don't match the ones on the vehicles still in his truck."

"What?" Mitch snapped. "That's impossible."

Greyson turned a cold eye on him and lifted the box Mitch had picked up from the craft store, the flaps on the lid swinging open. "Planning on doing a little Vehicle Identification Number etching, were you, Mr. Thompson?"

Oh fuck. What the hell had Katy bought? "No—I swear there's been a mistake."

Mackie shook his head as he grabbed Mitch's arm and escorted him from the building. "Then we'll sort it out down at the police station. Right now you're under arrest for suspicion of involvement with grand theft auto."

Chapter Seven

MITCH'S EXPRESSION remained stone cold as Anna waited behind the counter for him to be escorted from the holding cell he'd been stewing in for the past three hours.

Anna fought to keep from swaying, pushing aside the lightheaded rush that struck at seeing him in one piece. Her adrenaline count had to be off the charts—wakened from a solid sleep full of dirty sex dreams, she'd jerked on her clothes and hightailed it to Calgary as quickly as possible after Mitch had called.

Fortunately, showing her police identification had given her a chance to talk to the head officer of the raid. Detective Mackie had been more than reasonable, especially once they'd spotted the mix up on numbers between the manifest Mitch had presented and the bills of sale.

It was a mistake that would have been found eventually, but with the sheer number of arrests made that day it would have taken a lot longer to prove Mitch's innocence if she'd been someone off the street.

"You okay?" she asked Mitch as he joined her.

He dipped his head, but avoided meeting her eyes. "Do I need to do anything before we get the hell out of here?"

Detective Mackie rose from his desk, holding out a thin envelope. Mitch eyed it with suspicion. Anna grabbed the papers as Mackie explained. "Receipt for the items you brought in. I can't let you back into the yard today—you'll have to make another trip to pick up your transport. Sorry for the inconvenience, but the teams are working through there nonstop."

Mitch nodded then pushed past Anna to the exit door without another word.

Anna paused. "Thanks for your help, sir. I appreciate you taking the time to talk with me and help fix this mistake so quickly."

Mackie's gaze lingered on Mitch's back where he waited by the door, shoulders rigid under his jacket. "Let me know if there's anything else you need a hand with."

Mitch had to be watching, because he had the door open as soon as she was within touching distance. Only he didn't storm through like she expected, instead letting her step past him as he rotated to face the office.

"Detective Mackie?" Mitch called back.

The man looked up from where he'd returned to his paper-strewn desk. "Yes?"

"Thanks."

That was it. No waiting for a response, Mitch caught hold of her and pushed her before him, out of the building and into the parking lot.

Anna couldn't blame him for not wanting to stick around. "Come on, I parked over here."

She linked her fingers through his and tugged him in the right direction. He squeezed once, then let her lead. Silence accompanied their walk.

He grunted in surprise, though, when they turned the corner. "You drove my truck."

"You had a full tank of gas." She looked up at him. "I hope that was okay."

"Damn it, Anna." Mitch pulled her to a stop beside the driver's door and hauled her into his arms. The hold he had was less of an embrace and more as if he were drawing strength from the contact. Anna wove her arms around his waist and clung tightly. Waiting for him to get past the moment. Hoping he'd open up and talk...

Realizing that she wanted more intimacy—she wanted to know what he was feeling inside—and that knowledge turned her heart over in a weird flopping motion.

Mitch exhaled long and hard, his breath heating the side of her cheek. "Thank you for coming and getting me. Thanks for keeping my ass out of jail."

"You didn't do anything wrong, Mitch," Anna pointed out. "They would have found the proof eventually."

Mitch opened his door and gave her a hand in. "Eventually might have meant time behind bars, and trust me, I'm not game to repeat that experience ever again in my life."

He slid in after her and held out his hand.

Anna was in too much shock to understand what he was asking for at first. "Oh, your keys. Right here."

She dropped them into his palm before examining his face closely.

Mitch's dark eyes were pinned on hers. "You didn't know I got arrested once?"

She shook her head. "Too many speeding tickets?"

The side of his mouth twitched. Almost a smile. "I'm surprised you never heard about this. I was hanging out with a bunch of friends during high school, and things went a little too far. Playing chicken with their fathers' tractors ended badly—we destroyed property and the tractors. Unfortunately, one of the gang had pot in their pockets, so when the RCMP showed up and we all got hauled into the station we had that to deal with on top of it all. I ended up alone in a holding cell all night, and a juvvy arrest that's since been purged from the records."

"Wait—" *Alone*? "Where were the rest of the guys? And weren't your parents called?"

Mitch nodded even as he got them on the road and headed back north. "All our parents were. The rest of the group got bailed out, including the friend with drugs. Everyone, except me. Mom and Dad came to the station, found out what I'd been up to, then went home."

"Holy—really? That sounds so not like what I know of your Dad."

"I think if it had been Dad alone, he'd have caved, but my Mom—the woman had nerves of steel."

Anna twisted sideways on the bench seat to face Mitch. "You weren't even sixteen, right? If your mom was still around."

"Summer I was fifteen. Mom was already fighting cancer. She looked me in the eye and told me I could be anything I wanted to in life. And that some times things would happen that weren't fair, but that a lot of the time what happened to me would be a result of my actions."

"Consequences." Tough lesson to learn at any age. "So they left you overnight."

"Picked me up in the morning, took me out for the biggest breakfast I could eat. Told me they loved me, but if I ever got arrested again, they'd be damn disappointed."

He shut up then, lips pressed tight, both hands clutching the wheel tight as if he needed his full concentration to drive. Anna stared out the window for a bit, letting the warm air from the heater blow over them as she leaned against his side. The miles flew past, the sunlight shining on the wintery wonderland already growing fainter. Days were getting shorter all the time.

Time sped past. A steady blur of night and day, more work and more play, but all of it spinning together and mixing into one grey mass that was indistinguishable from the next.

The never-ending forward roll right now made her wonder where exactly she was headed. She had her job, in spite of the frustrations. She had her family, no matter that they weren't always on the same page.

The goals she'd set over the past years didn't feel like enough anymore.

Because of Mitch…

Where was this going? Was this going anywhere, the relationship between the two of them? He'd said he wanted more, and that the physical side wasn't enough.

Mitch was a good man. He had a family who loved him and cared for him. He had things he was passionate about, more than just burning up the highway on his bike.

He was opening up more as time passed—and there was that theme again. A constant loop in her brain. Time *was* passing. In the end, things would be different than they were now.

Where was this going? What did she want?

Could she offer him more than what he already had?

"Why did you call me, Mitch?"

He stiffened, and Anna kicked herself. The question had come out of the blue for him. She softened her tone and caught his arm carefully. "I mean, I'm glad you did, but..."

"Why not one of the boys?" He cracked a real smile for the first time since she'd picked him up. "Can you imagine giving them this kind of ammunition to hold over me during every fight from now to eternity?"

Anna held his arm reassuringly.

Mitch glanced at her. "I knew I hadn't done anything wrong, and I hoped you'd be able to help me. I'm sorry if that was taking advantage of what we've got happening."

"Of course it wasn't. I'm glad it was so simple to spot what had gone wrong."

There was a short pause before he spoke softly. "Can we keep this on the quiet? I don't want to upset Katy."

Oh. Katy must have been the one who wrote down the wrong numbers. "When Mackie and I went through them, we found the bills of sale were correct, and there were only a couple digits slipped in other places."

Mitch nodded. "And if it had been a normal day, with a normal parts drop, that kind of mix-up would have meant nothing. We would have found the mistake when Denis and I went over the papers, compared them to the bills of sale, and fixed things. Done."

"It was the raid that complicated matters." She was glad they had found all the missing details. "You guys picked a good salvage yard for selling off parts," Anna teased lightly.

He shook his head. "Years it's been that we've used that place. Denis has been rock solid for *years*. I can't figure out what the hell he was thinking setting up a chop shop."

"Tight times means people sometimes make stupid mistakes. Or greed—thinking it's easy money." She squeezed his thigh. "I'm sorry you got caught in the middle of it."

"Anyway, I don't want Katy to know. I'll obviously tell Dad we need a new salvage yard, but she doesn't need more on her plate right now. Not with everything she's dealing with after the accident."

His devotion to his family caused a lump to rise in Anna's throat. She deliberately bumped him with her shoulder. "Tell her what?"

Finally a laugh escaped him, even though it was a small one. "You're golden. Thanks."

"Hey, all charges were dropped, which means it never happened," she pointed out.

Mitch draped an arm around her shoulders and hauled her in as close as possible. "Sorry if I was a little abrupt back at the station. I swore I'd never get into a situation where I'd be arrested again, and I never have. Hated to get caught up just because of a mistake."

Anna offered another squeeze. "You didn't do anything wrong. That was proven. Try to forget it."

He fell silent, only this time it was a more comfortable silence. Anna turned up the radio, cuddled into his side and got lost in her thoughts.

They drove for over an hour before making a pit stop for gas and drinks. Mitch cracked open his coke while

Anna twisted off the cap of her drink and peeked under the lid. She snorted in derision before she could stop herself.

"What's so funny?" he demanded.

"It says 'You will journey to your heart's desire'. The only journeying I currently have planned doesn't involve my heart's desire." If she could even figure out what that was. Anna shook her head then took a long drink of the sweet orange liquid.

"Hey, don't knock it," Mitch said. "Maybe you'll get a chance to go to some great conference for work."

While interesting, she doubted that was her heart's desire. "If it's held in Hawaii, I'm game."

"Maybe you'll win some hot-shot constable-of-the-year thing for all your hard work. They appreciate you at the station." Mitch stroked her shoulder lightly. "I think you're pretty awesome."

His touch was doing things that shouldn't be allowed with so little effort. "Mitch. Eyes on the road."

"Just checking my rearview mirror, Constable." He wasn't looking out the back window though, his expression turning lustful. "Your tits are showing."

Anna laughed, and suddenly the tension drained away like they'd pulled a plug, splashing anxiety and fear behind them as they closed in on Rocky Mountain House.

A wicked urge hit, and she loosened off her coat, dropping it on the passenger seat.

Mitch kept his gaze forward, both hands back on the wheel, but the glances to the side increased in tempo. "What're you doin'?"

Anna pulled her hair loose from the ponytail she'd had it in, fluffing out the long strands. "Getting comfy."

Next, two buttons on her shirt slipped through easy enough, and if he'd caught a glimpse of cleavage before, there was now a lot more for him to enjoy.

"Jesus," Mitch muttered, but other than that, he didn't respond.

She leaned in, resting her breasts against his arm as she kissed his cheek lightly. "I'm glad everything worked out today. And I'm very glad you called me. Thank you for trusting me."

With one finger she stroked a line down his neck, smiling as he swallowed hard enough it showed. She continued the tease downward, along his shoulder, over his biceps. A small wiggle allowed her to slip her palm against his chest, nestling in tight enough that his rapidly beating heart echoed in her ear.

She skirted his groin, instead resting her palm on his thigh. "When we get home?"

He cleared his throat. "Yeah?" The word was barely audible. Lust-filled.

Breathless.

"When we get home I think you should stop in the yard. We'll just sit in the truck for a bit so I can pull out your cock and suck it."

Mitch gurgled.

"I don't want you to take off your jeans, just open them up and lift your cock out. Hmm, I love looking at your piercing. At how those gold balls look against the smooth skin when you're excited. So thick I can barely hold you in my mouth."

He shifted his hips, and Anna lowered her voice, easing her lips toward his ear so their bodies were pressed together as she breathed the words.

"Or maybe we will get rid of your pants, because then I can reach your balls. Play with them while I'm jacking you off. My fist around you, my mouth on just the head of your cock. Teasing with you with my tongue until you can't see straight."

"Sweet mercy, Anna..."

She was barely touching him, but the truck cab was steaming hot.

And filled with blue and red light.

Anna whipped her head around and swore as a familiar RCMP cruiser came into sight. Mitch echoed her, damn near synchronized in their cussing, which only made their tension turn to laughter.

"I'm so sorry," she gasped as he pulled over to the side. "I shouldn't have distracted you."

He reached across the seat and opened the glove box while they waited, leaning hard against her as he pulled out his papers. "Just remember what you were talking about, because holy fuck, I'm holding you to that."

When he rolled down his window and Nick's stern face popped into view, Anna felt like cursing all over again.

"You had anything to drink this afterno—" Nick froze as he spotted her. "Oh."

Thank God, Mitch answered the question as if there'd been no interruption. "No, sir. No alcohol. I wasn't speeding, was I?"

Nick dragged his gaze away, his cheeks flushed red. That's when she remembered the open buttons on her blouse. She bit the inside of her cheek, although she wasn't sure if it was to stop from screaming or laughing.

Her partner cleared his throat. "No, you were within proper speed limits, but you were weaving down the road. I suggest you concentrate on your driving a little harder, Mr. Thompson. I'll let you off with a warning, but next time I'll have to give you a ticket for distracted driving."

He dipped his head at Anna before escaping back to the cruiser, his pace slowing to a more professional saunter almost instantly.

Mitch glanced at Anna. "Maybe next time you should drive."

She poked him in the side. "Get us home."

The flash of fire in his eyes was the Mitch she knew. Knew and...

Too soon.

It was too soon, but time was passing. What was her heart's desire? Until she figured that out, time would still keep moving forward, whether or not she moved with it.

Chapter Eight

"WE'RE GOING *where?*"

Mitch ignored the shock in her voice. "Cassidy's place."

Anna's gaze narrowed. "Cassidy's place is the same as saying my cousin Travis's place. Dude, if you think for a single second I'm doing anything remotely kinky while my cousin is in the room, you can go to hell."

"That attitude is going to severely curtail our sex life. It's tough to go anywhere in this town without one of your cousins popping up," Mitch teased.

She laughed, the sound escaping reluctantly. "There're not that many of us, but we do seem to get around. But back to the point, what gives?"

"Cassidy and Ashley invited us over, that's all." Which was true but only by the barest of definitions.

It had been nearly two months since he'd convinced her to turn their sexual trysts into something more. Two weeks since she'd rescued his ass from the police station, and he'd been trying his damnedest to keep them moving forward. Only between her work and the usual insanity of the garage, they hadn't had much time together. Not nearly as much as he'd hoped for.

Mitch wondered at times if all the strange shift changes Anna got had something to do with Nick. The cold looks from the bastard any time the two of them met in Rocky were enough to freeze Mitch's ass.

It was clear the man didn't approve of him, only Mitch wasn't sure if there was more to it than that. He fought the shot of jealousy that struck as he thought of all the time Nick got to spend with Anna.

He needed a distraction. He needed her warmth. Tonight? They were going to work on her list.

"Travis is out of town. He's helping his brother Daniel drive a load of furniture to Banff this weekend, so you won't even see your cousin."

She relaxed, facing the front window again as the winter scenery flew past. "Nice to have new people settling into the area."

"Cassidy is a rock. I enjoyed the time he worked with us in the garage before he got on with the Coleman ranch. And Ashley is…" He couldn't stop his lips from twisting into a smile.

Anna tapped her elbow against his side. "Guys turn into such hound dogs around her. Go on. You're allowed to say it. She's hot."

"She's a firecracker, but she's also very taken. By two guys." He squeezed her thigh. "And I've got my own flamethrower right here."

Anna winked. "Good recovery, but it doesn't change things. I know what I've heard about Ashley. The woman has a mind of her own when it comes to being sexually liberated. I think she's what people call a free spirit."

He debated how much to tell Anna, but full disclosure seemed the safest plan. "I talked to Cass about one of the things on your fantasy list," he confessed.

He glanced sideways in time to see her cheeks bloom crimson. "Great. Do I have to guess which one?"

"I think you can figure it out. But we don't have to do anything," he assured her. "Only if you're comfortable, Cass is onboard."

Anna paused. "You said Cassidy and Ashley would be home."

Mitch nodded slowly. "Well, Cassidy obviously had to ask what his partners thought of the proposal. Travis didn't mind but had to be out of the picture, but Ashley…"

"Go on."

"Ashley thought it sounded damn hot and insisted she wanted to be there as well."

"Oh, *jeez.*"

Mitch pulled over to the side of the road so he could cup her chin in his hand and look her in the eye. "Nothing happens you don't want to, but Ashley's right. It's fucking hot to consider watching Ashley and Cassidy fool around. They think watching us would be hot as well. That's it. Nothing more."

"Watching only? No touching?" Anna clarified before rolling her eyes. "God, I can't believe I asked that. I feel like a deviant."

"Bullshit—you're not being a deviant to enjoy life. We're not proposing a free-for-all or a gangbang between people who don't give a shit about anything other than getting their own rocks off. We're two adults who know what we like. They're two adults with a consenting third partner. They don't want to break the commitment

87

they've made to each other, but we all agreed watching is fine. It's like…live-action porn in a safe place, and no one but us will ever know."

Anna still hesitated. "It sounds so contrived now that we've had to plan it out."

"I figured if I *didn't* plan it you'd put my balls in a vise."

She snorted. He was probably right.

Mitch leaned in and pressed his lips to hers. A slow, thorough kiss that started soft, then advanced rapidly into lots of tongue and heavy breathing. He was gratified to feel the knot of tension in her shoulders melting away as heat rose between them.

Anna pulled back reluctantly. "Stop it. We're going to get a citation for public indecency."

Mitch winked, then put the truck back in gear and continued down the road. "Think of it this way. The possibility is there. If nothing happens, that's fine. We'll shoot the bull for a while, have a few laughs—there's no agenda, Anna. Just a night out with a couple friends."

"A couple friends we might get naked in front of."

A shiver shook her, and Mitch waited to see if she'd say anything else. Admit to anything else. He was pretty sure the idea turned her on damn hard, but he wasn't going to push.

If she decided they call the whole thing off, he'd be fine with that as well.

Cassidy met them at the front door. The trio had moved into the old Peter's house on the Six Pack land— one of the earliest homesteads in the Rocky Mountain House area, and the origin of the Coleman ranch. The house was in the process of renovations, but there was still plenty of room to join Cassidy on the front porch.

His blond hair stuck up every which way as if he'd recently gotten out of the shower. "Come on in and ignore the mess. I'm running late, and Ashley is even later."

Anna hesitated in the doorway. "You want us to come back some other time?"

Cassidy shook his head, briefly shaking hands with Mitch. "Nah. I just got caught out in the fields later than usual. I'm still learning the lay of the land. Your cousin Matt and I were about fifteen miles farther north than I expected, chasing down some runaway horses."

"And Ashley?" Mitch asked, stepping behind Anna and stroking the back of her neck softly with his fingertips.

A full-out grin escaped Cassidy. "She's in her studio getting projects ready for her rescheduled art show. If we didn't haul her out of there occasionally, she'd forget to eat, sleep or do anything human until she's done."

They all laughed. Anna leaned into Mitch, a small but subtle shift. "Nice that she enjoys what she's doing so much."

Cassidy grabbed a coat off the wall hooks and shrugged it on. "Come on, I'll show you the studio. You can take a peek, and after we can pull her away from her work."

"She won't mind?" Mitch asked.

"Nope. Ashley likes an audience."

Mitch held back his snort of laughter as he exchanged glances with Anna. She looked about ready to burst, but she slipped her fingers into his and they followed Cassidy around the back of the house to a two-storey old barn.

"The house renovations aren't done because me and Travis fixed this up first," Cassidy explained as he pushed open the door, closing it quickly after them to block out the icy December air. The scent of paint and turpentine hung around them, along with the fresher aroma of cedar boards and pine boughs. A heavy beat echoed off the walls, music playing loudly from somewhere over their heads.

The level they were on held a small workspace with a sink along one wall and a two-burner stovetop, but mostly it seemed to be storage. Rows and rows of shelving, some covered with boxes, others still empty. Light poured down from above, showcasing the stairs leading to the second level. Cassidy took the steps two at a time as he moved ahead of them. "Hey, Ash, you got company," he shouted.

"...chills. Oh, baby, ooooohhhh..."

Mitch squeezed Anna's hand. "She sings too."

"Stop it." Anna laughed as she tugged him up the stairs, warm air pouring over them from a ceiling mounted heater.

They paused at the top of the landing, and Anna was struck with how well the guys had designed the workspace. Unless someone stood on one of the distant hills behind the shop and used binoculars, the second-storey space was a nearly perfect private oasis.

The upper floor had no interior walls, only a wide-open space from ceiling to peaked roof. Fading sunlight shone in the exterior windows that faced the back fields of the Coleman property, but most of the brightness at this time of day came from a bank of suspended ceiling lights strategically placed to spotlight Ashley's main work area.

The artist in question stood behind an oversized canvas, pretty much hidden from view, but she was audible, singing at the top of her lungs along with the music she had cranked to eleven.

"...oh, yeah, do it. Do me, baby..."

Cassidy twisted down the volume, and Ashley's blonde head suddenly appeared, followed by the rest of her. Anna's hand tightened in Mitch's as they realized Ashley was dressed in her underwear and nothing else.

"Hey, lover." Ashley put down her paintbrush and stepped across the sturdy wood floorboards, her hand held out. "Perfect timing. Take off your clothes."

Cassidy cleared his throat, grabbing a robe from where it was draped over the back of a nearby chair. "Ash, we have guests, remember?"

She blinked hard, as if pulling herself back from some other place, then Ashley smiled sweetly at them. "Hey, guys. Sorry, I need to borrow Cassidy for about five minutes. I can't figure out what I've done wrong here. Come see."

She slipped her arms into the robe absentmindedly as Cassidy helped her. Mitch found her attractive, but he was far more interested in seeing Anna get naked, her curves the ones he craved.

Still, it was an interesting start to what could be a *very* interesting evening. Mitch let Anna lead him to where Cassidy and Ashley waited.

THE WELL-LIT studio made Anna feel as if she were standing under a spotlight. Not only exposed on the outside but in, as if the shadows in her character were also being peered into. No hiding anywhere.

She'd asked for this evening, and Mitch had delivered—if she was brave enough to go along for the ride.

"Ash," Cassidy protested, his hands covering his girlfriend's.

"Oh, come on." Ashley tugged his T-shirt free from his pants, her fingers going for the button on his jeans. "I don't have the right anatomy to check in the mirror. I tried, but I need dude muscles."

"Is that why you were painting in your underwear?" Cassidy asked, stepping back from her.

"Yes. *Pleeeease...*" she wheedled.

He offered an apologetic shrug to Anna and Mitch. "You mind?"

Anna shook her head, then stepped closer to examine Ashley's painting. "What's the problem? Not that I can help—I'm not artsy."

"This line here." Ashley pointed to the painting. "See? I got his chest right, I know I have, but that Adonis muscle...I'm not positive how much it crunches when he's picking up a saddle."

The partially finished portrait on the canvas was going to be gorgeous. In the foreground was a cowboy, his horse waiting behind him to be saddled, fence rails and rolling foothills as a backdrop.

"Well, I don't usually pick up saddles when I'm half-naked, so that's one problem you've got off the bat," Cassidy teased.

Ashley stuck out her tongue. "Bend over and reach for the floor."

"Pretend you dropped the soap," Mitch drawled, and Cassidy burst out laughing, swinging a finger in Mitch's direction.

"Bad boys." Ashley pouted. "I'm trying to make art, and you're getting dirty."

"You like dirty," Cassidy commented as he obediently got back into position, his work-hardened body pretty damn easy on the eyes. "Welcome to the nuthouse, Anna. Aren't you glad you came?"

Mitch curled himself around her so he could whisper in her ear. "You'll be even gladder once you come, right?"

Her cheeks flushed.

Watching. Being watched. Right now she couldn't decide which thought was causing goose bumps to rise over her entire body. Making her nipples pebble without a direct touch.

Ashley drew some firm pencil lines on the canvas, rubbing with her fingertips to add shadows. "Perfect."

"Thank you." Cassidy straightened up and closed in on her. "Now are you done?"

The short pause while he kissed her gave enough time for Mitch to sneak his hand over Anna's belly, thumb teasing in circles as they watched Ashley twine her fingers into Cassidy's hair and thoroughly get into the kiss.

Mitch stood at her back, a solid mass of man that she was itching to touch all over. When he slipped his hand under her shirt so he was rubbing bare skin, she moaned softly.

His touch was addictive.

Ashley pulled back from Cassidy, smiling contentedly at him before turning toward her guests.

"There's one more thing…" She spoke quietly. "And feel free to say no, but, Mitch? You've got tattoos."

He gasped in shock. "Oh my God, really?"

Anna elbowed him, and he laughed as she muttered, "Behave."

Ashley stepped closer. "I'm designing a tattoo for a friend. I've never done that before, and I want to make sure I account for how curvature might affect what I draw. You mind?"

There was heat in his eyes as he glanced at Anna. Not for permission, per se, more as a warning. "I'll take off mine if you take off yours."

The game changed. All the oxygen sucked out of the room.

Anna focused on Mitch alone, staring into his dark eyes as he took a leisurely perusal of her from top to bottom. "You daring me, Thompson?"

"Since when does a Coleman need to be dared to get dirty?"

She stepped closer, deliberately ignoring Ashley and Cassidy. Acutely aware they were there. She could still see them in her peripheral vision. Cassidy moved to the sidewall, and the bright lights shining on them dimmed to almost nothing.

Mitch pulled off his T-shirt, dropping it over the back of the wooden chair beside him. Muscles flexed as he stretched lazily, chest muscles bulging, biceps molding into rocks. The tattoos curling and extending with his motions like living creatures.

Anna planted her feet on either side of his, close enough their body heat meshed. "You want skin? You got it."

She caught the bottom of her shirt and lifted it without bothering to undo the buttons. The fabric teased her skin as it rose, a soft brush of cotton that raced up her spine like fingers.

Only right now no one was touching her. Just Mitch's dark gaze eating her up.

And a low hum of approval from where Ashley and Cassidy stood.

The sound broke the spell Anna had been weaving around herself. Made it impossible to pretend she and Mitch were alone. That was fine, though, because as Mitch trailed his fingers down her collarbone, the sensation that followed was that much more because they *weren't* alone.

Her awareness was cranked to maximum. Not only in how she responded to Mitch pressing his full palm around her ribs, fingers spread wide as he caressed her back. Not only the sounds in the air—their breathing becoming more rapid, small noises of pleasure escaping from both groups. Her blood pounded through her veins—she felt every pulse, felt her pussy getting wetter in anticipation of being taken.

Alive, like she'd never been before.

Mitch thumbed her bra hooks open, pressing a kiss to her shoulder as he skimmed the thin straps down. He eased back far enough for the cups to fall away, and she was naked from the waist up, his hands cupping the full globes of her breasts. The aching need for him only increased, and he winked, only a second, and put his lips to her skin.

Kisses at first then his tongue, tracing a line down her neck before heading lower. He paused only enough to grab a wooden chair and drop into it, pulling her into his lap and trapping her hips in position over the thick length of his engorged cock.

That controlling hand had returned to her lower back. Holding her in place as he slid his other hand up to lightly collar her throat.

The delicate pressure he exerted pushed her into an arch, and the next thing she knew he'd wrapped his lips around her nipple. Wet heat, the sharp bite of his teeth. Anna shuddered hard enough the chair under them skittered on the hardwood floor.

"So damn beautiful," Mitch whispered. "Your skin is flushing, body softening. If I put my fingers into you right now, I bet you'd drench me."

"Do it." Anna deliberately opened her eyes and curled upright, reaching for her button and wiggling off his lap.

Mitch grinned. "Eager, are you?"

She was about to explode, and he was asking stupid questions. "You want me to do it myself?"

Instant lust ripped over his expression, and Anna found herself twirled then pinned to his hard body. The rough stubble on his cheek scratched her cheek and shoulder as he leaned them together. "There's no rush. Ashley wants to see my ink. Let's give her a clean canvas to contrast them against."

Again, one of his hands went up, the other down. Both barely touching her, but the minute hairs on her skin stood straight on end. His top arm cradled her torso, his wide-spread fingers cupping her breast, thumb teasing back and forth over her nipple.

With his other hand, he finished what she'd started. Unzipped her pants then shoved them down far enough to reveal her panties.

He was right—she was soaking wet already, and only getting wetter the longer he delayed.

The bold lines of his tattoos curled around his arms like he was curled around her, the flames against her pale skin making it appear she was the one on fire.

She was. Inside and out. An incinerator had been lit in her belly that was melting away all restraint and inhibitions. Anna took a deep breath then peeked under her lashes toward Cassidy and Ashley's corner.

The two of them were tangled together as well. Ashley had lost the robe, and not only was Cassidy's chest still bare, his pants were open. Ashley had his cock in her hand and was stroking him.

But both of them were watching Mitch and Anna with an unwavering focus.

Anna wasn't sure what she'd expected to feel, knowing for certain Mitch's caresses were being witnessed. As he slid his fingers into her panties and Ashley's gaze followed, Anna's only response was to open her legs as wide as her half-dropped pants would allow.

There should have been some embarrassment, maybe, to accompany the illicit thrill. But with Cassidy's gaze fixed on her chest, and Mitch rocking his cock against her lower back, she was overwhelmed with that internal fire. Heat licking through her like she'd gone molten inside.

Mitch parted her folds. "I'm going to fingerfuck you. Then once you've had an orgasm or two, I'll bend you over this chair and fuck you for real."

"*Yes.*" Anna clutched his wrist as he thrust into her. She was wet, so he didn't hold back. Thick fingers shoved deep, and she dropped her head back on his shoulder and moaned as he pulled out so slowly she felt every second with an intensity that rocked her.

Mitch released her for long enough to shove her pants to the floor, setting his hands on her hips and ripping the edge of her panties apart. Then he was back, her legs kicked farther apart, her body arching as he drew her upright and set his hands back on her.

This time when he drove his fingers in and started fucking her, he didn't stop. Not until she was shaking, cries escaping her lips. Through half-closed eyes she focused across the room on Cassidy and Ashley. He had Ashley bent over his arm, his cock buried in her pussy as they pulsed together. Erotic to watch, intoxicating.

Anna would have been envious, but there was no time, because her orgasm swept in and swept her away. Sex clutching tight around Mitch, the wet sounds of his fingers pumping deep into her mixing with the other sex noises in the room.

Mitch was already changing their position. He didn't take her over the chair like he'd suggested he would, though. Instead he sat again, his jeans shoved away, his cock upright and waiting for her, the golden flash of his piercing catching the light.

Anna didn't hesitate. She went eagerly as he lifted her over him, reaching down to guide his hard shaft between her folds. The instant she let him go, Mitch thrust upward and she screamed his name. The hard balls of his piercing added an extra touch that made stars float before her eyes.

It didn't matter who was in the room right then or what they were doing. Low groans from Cassidy and squeaks of happiness from Ashley—all of that faded away because nothing compared to what Mitch was doing.

He held her hips and controlled her, pounding her with his cock as their lips met. Hungry kisses, breathless gasping. Everything inside coiling tighter and tighter until there was nothing and nowhere to go except up in flames.

"Mitch, oh God, *oh...*" Anna rocked hard, their bodies only kept together by the strong grip he held on her. She buried her face against his neck and let herself be braced in place. Fully supported as her climax ripped her brain clear out of her head, and all thought became impossible.

Mitch froze, her hips tight to his thighs, his cock jerking inside her. "Fucking hell, that was so..." He gasped for air, panting in her ear as their bodies slicked together. Sweaty and sated.

Her eyes met his, her voice a mere whisper. "I can't move."

He laughed softly. Fingers trailing up her spine and teasing her. He kissed her forehead. "Then don't. There's nowhere we need to go."

In the corner Cassidy and Ashley were curled up together, talking quietly. Mostly naked, and not in the least concerned by that fact. They kissed and nuzzled each other with such honest love and affection, and something deep inside Anna cracked open with longing.

Mitch was giving her all her sexual fantasies. Could he give her what she needed most? She watched the couple across the room and listened to the steady beat of Mitch's heart.

And wondered.

Chapter Nine

LAUGHTER RANG over the heavy beat of the music. Mitch turned away from the group gathered by the dance floor and tapped his fingers impatiently on the table, sipping his beer between moments of glancing at his watch.

Anna was late. Again. He'd bet big money that it would be Nick's doing. The man seemed determined to mess with Anna's time, and along with it, Mitch and Anna's relationship. Mitch didn't know if he should be jealous along with the frustration.

A heavy beat pounded in his chest as Anna finally strutted in.

"*Jesus,*" Mitch moaned, rising to his feet, accidentally kicking his chair over as he took in her outfit.

Her hair was coiled into a fancier-than-usual ponytail that he looked forward to messing up. A wraparound sweater clung to all her curves, the bottom edge stopping mere inches above her skirt line.

The skirt itself wasn't that short—not really—but enough of her legs were exposed to make his mouth water, and the entire smooth length led to those drop-dead shoes he loved. Mitch couldn't take his gaze off the straps of red leather on her feet.

Fuck, she'd worn the shoes.

Something inside stood and cheered. The rest of him just got harder than a spike. Since the night at Cassidy's, it was as if she'd let loose the woman he'd seen small glimpses of forever. That passionate side came out far more often now, visible in the daytime as well as in the secret moments they'd steal together.

The smaller than usual Tuesday night crowd pivoted to watch Anna glide toward him. She ignored them, fixated on his face. She must have seen something she liked, because a smile escaped. A flirty, naughty smile as she stepped right into his arms and kissed him.

Mitch was the one to hold back, because his first impulse was to wrap her leg around his hip and start dry humping her right there in the middle of the fucking bar.

Screw sitting and talking. He wanted her in his arms where she belonged. He slipped his fingers over her hip and guided her straight to the dance floor. "Come here."

Anna settled against him, one leg on either side of his as she pressed close. "Not even going to buy me a drink first, sailor?"

"You already got my cock so fucking hard I can't sit down," Mitch confessed.

Her dirty chuckle in response only stoked the flames higher. So be it. Mitch rested his hands on her ass and pulled up tight until there wasn't a lick of breathing room between them.

Music and voices blended together into the background as Mitch stared into her eyes. Anna draped her arms around his shoulders, her fingers teasing the short hairs at the back of his neck. The expression she wore couldn't be considered anything but a smirk.

"You're looking damn pleased." Mitch slipped one hand farther around to the center of her lower back. "I love the shoes, but this sweater has got to go. I'd prefer you in a short T-shirt so I can get my hands on bare skin."

"Just enjoy rubbing that soft fabric instead." Anna hummed happily, her hip grazing his dick as she shifted position. "God, you are hard, aren't you. Poor man."

"Jeez. Do that again, and I'll flip you over my fucking knee right here, right now."

Her tongue darted out, leaving behind a shimmer of moisture on the pouting surface of her lower lip. "I don't think so. I think you're going to buy me a drink first. Then we can talk about fucking on our knees."

Mitch laughed. The song ended, and she dragged him to one of the tall tables lining the dance-floor perimeter. Easy conversation followed over a drink. Laughter and dirty talk. All the time, Anna was never so far away from him that some part of their bodies wasn't in contact.

He was going to explode if he didn't take a breather soon. Or take her home and bury himself in her sweet body for the rest of the night. "Keep that thought," Mitch interrupted their discussion. "I'll be right back."

He hit the can, more to regain control than anything. After splashing cold water on his face, he dragged his wet hand over the back of his neck. Checked in the mirror only to see proof his expression was as hungry as his gut warned him.

She did things to him he couldn't control. Hell, things he didn't *want* to control, and that was the trouble.

Only three steps outside the door, he slammed into a woman exiting the ladies' room. Mitch grabbed on tight, familiar soft material gliding under his fingers.

"Shit, sorry." Anna wrapped her fingers around his biceps as she regained her balance.

It was too tempting. Mitch twirled her, crowding forward until her back hit the wall. "Time to pay a toll," he quipped.

Then his mouth was on hers, his tongue dipping between her lips. The front of his body pressed her to the wall, his cock nestled over the V of her legs.

She gave as good as she got, writhing against him, her breathing picking up as she tangled her fingers in his hair. Mitch twisted slightly to one side so he could drop a hand to her leg, easing around and dragging his fingers along the soft flesh on her inner thigh.

Anna gasped for air as he brushed her panties, thumb unerringly striking her clit. "Jesus, woman. You're soaking wet," Mitch whispered.

"Mitch, *oh...*"

He closed his fingers on the hard little nub of her clit again, pinching enough that her head fell back to the wall leaving room for him to attack her bare neck. He worked his way up to her ear, speaking quietly but frantically. "Take me home, or I swear I'm turning you around and riding you right here."

She didn't get a chance to respond.

"Ahem."

The shock of the sound pulled Mitch back from the brink of lust.

Anna's sharp gasp warned him more than the sight of the somewhat familiar man behind them. Mitch blocked the view as much as possible while he smoothed her skirt and allowed her to compose herself.

The extra time to let his cock stop trying to leap out of his jeans was also needed.

The man cleared his throat again. "Anna."

Her fingers were still curled into the material of Mitch's shirt, only now not in passion, but in fear. "Stewart."

Oh shit—Mitch recognized that name. One of her coworkers.

Stewart didn't look away as Anna stepped from behind Mitch, her chin held high by sheer willpower. The RCMP's gaze dropped, lingering on the exposed length of legs and the fiery red shoes before returning to assess Mitch. Eyeing the distance between the two of them. It seemed Stewart hadn't missed the way Mitch surreptitiously slid his hand out of Anna's skirt, and the visible disapproval in the man's eyes filled Mitch with unease.

Nothing more was said before Stewart pushed past them into the men's room.

Anna's head hit the wall behind her with a far-too-solid thud. "Oh, God."

Mitch skimmed his hand down her arm and linked their fingers together. "Sorry if I got you in shit."

She took a deep breath and let it out slowly. "We got ourselves in shit." Anna leaned her forehead on his chest briefly before squeezing his hand and tugging him forward. "Come on. One more dance for the road before we go home."

Holding her chastely in his arms was a huge change after the feverish pitch they'd built up to, but Mitch still enjoyed it, except for the concern over being damn near caught in the act. He trailed his fingers over her back and attempted to soothe out the tension.

Stewart paused on the edge of the room and watched them for a minute before disappearing, and Mitch hoped like hell that any troubles would vanish along with him.

IT WAS too much to hope that nothing would come of her and Mitch's indiscretion the previous night. The phone on her desk rang the instant Anna walked into her office. She stared at it as if it were going to bite her. The coming turmoil was her own damn fault. Time to face the consequences.

Staff Sergeant Max was brief as he summoned her to his office.

She double-checked her uniform before pacing down the hall, the long walk feeling far too reminiscent of the one and only time she'd been called to the principal's office.

Only this time she feared the consequences would be more than detention.

The staff sergeant stood by the window, his back to her as she entered. "Sit down, Constable Coleman."

Anna pulled a chair to the side and lowered herself gingerly, fighting the urge to burst out with apologies or explanations. She wasn't going to leap to conclusions concerning exactly where this conversation would go.

The knot in her stomach wasn't about to get any smaller, though. Not until she knew.

"Constable Stewart spoke with me earlier today." No preamble. The staff sergeant pivoted, a stern look set in place, including a furrow between his brows. "I have to admit, I was disappointed to hear what he had to share."

Her lips hurt from pressing them together.

Max sighed heavily. "The good news is he insists you were not so far out of line that you deserve to receive a formal reprimand, but I'm afraid I'm torn. I don't want to put anything on your permanent record that's going to harm your career, but public indecency isn't the way to make a good impression."

"No, sir." The words whispered past the tightness in her throat. This was so not good.

Her superior officer folded his arms. "Even when you're not in uniform, you're still being watched. You're still representing your position. The heat of passion needs to be controlled, Constable."

The situation was as bad as having a discussion about sex with her mother when she was a teenager. "Yes, sir. It was inappropriate, and it won't happen again."

"I don't expect my staff to be cookie cutters. I expect you all to have different interests and hobbies. Relationships outside of work." He met Anna's eyes and wouldn't let her look away. "But being involved in legal dirt biking is one thing, lewd acts in public is another. Especially since you're the liaison for the high school students. There's an even higher expectation of moral control expected, something I thought well within your capabilities."

She had to fight to stop from cringing. She'd been surprised how much she was actually enjoying working with the kids. Having unwittingly jeopardized that position increased her guilt.

"Was I wrong about you, Constable?" Staff Sergeant Max demanded.

"No, sir." She didn't offer any excuses, because there were none she could give.

He stared at her for a solid minute before nodding. "I'm going to put a note in your file, Anna. A personal reprimand that I will remove after a reasonable amount of time. What do you think?"

She thought she was going to fall over, the relief was so strong. "I won't disappoint you again, sir."

"See that you don't. If there's another incident, of any sort, I'll have no choice but to follow official guidelines, including misdemeanor charges if appropriate. I hope I'm making myself clear."

Anna tangled her fingers together tighter to stop from fidgeting. "You are. Perfectly."

He dismissed her, and she paced back to her desk, pulling out work and spreading it on the surface. Her eyes barely focusing on the pages before her.

Remorse at her actions rushed her. It wasn't the relationship with Mitch she regretted, but loosening her carefully held control too far. What she'd done wasn't horrifyingly wrong, only getting caught *was* complicated by her job.

The idea of anything tearing apart what she'd worked so hard for made her ill. The fact it was her own damn fault was even worse.

A strange numbness set in as she wondered how to deal with this—the next steps. Because while she didn't want to give up her career, she didn't want to give up the changes in her life since she'd started seeing Mitch.

Going back would be like closing a part of herself into an icy-cold storage, and she didn't know if she could do that.

The only good part was that she didn't have to make her next decision alone. She sent a text to Mitch, asking to meet that evening. Right now she had no idea what even to suggest. She sank into work and let it distract her.

MITCH CRANKED up the heater in his truck a notch and cursed the weather. Early December wasn't supposed to be this cold, but they were stuck in a hellish deep freeze. Not even halfway through the month, and the cold snap that had set in was breaking records.

In some ways, Mitch didn't mind. He had the warm garage to work in, and the hotter-than-hell moments with Anna. The moments spent with her were truly becoming the highlights of his week, and wasn't that the most goddamn, pathetic, pussy-whipped thing.

If any of his brothers had a girl they were this besotted with, he'd be tormenting them night and day. As it was, the guys were too into their own heads at the moment to even notice Mitch's obsession. Dealing in their own ways with their concern over their little sister, and the missing parts of their lives.

Mitch adjusted the heater again, blasting hot air toward his feet while he considered the truth. For a close-knit family, they were still a bunch of tight-lipped individuals. Not even their regular Thursday-night family dinner seemed to change that.

Of course, some of the secret-keeping made sense. Like after his little incident at the salvage yard. Clay had been the one to grab the company truck from the impound lot, saving Mitch the trip back to the scene of the crime. Between Clay, Mitch and their dad, they'd kept Katy and the younger guys from finding out anything had gone sideways. Just announced Thompson and Sons were using a new yard in the future, and that was that.

Such a simple solution to what could have become a huge deal. He hoped the current cluster-fuck with Anna's work would settle out as smoothly.

The final stretch of highway appeared ahead of him. The long trip to pick up supplies at the border had eaten up his entire day when all he really wanted was to get back to Anna. Other than the one text message, she hadn't called, and he didn't want to interrupt her.

Dusk turned the world around him into a surreal murder mystery, or post-apocalyptic wasteland, painting the snowfields red and grey. Dark clouds hovering above the treetops warned of an approaching snowstorm. Even the strange beauty couldn't distract him from his goal, though, as his anxiety increased.

He needed to get home to find out what had happened with Anna.

He'd just turned the corner off the main highway, headed toward Rocky, when flashing lights once again showed up in his rearview mirror.

Mitch cursed loudly, eyeing his speedometer. What the hell? He knew it wasn't Anna pulling him over for a joke, because she was at his place waiting for him, and there was no way he'd been speeding.

If it had been sixty seconds later, he might have been caught with his foot to the floorboards. This section of highway was straight and smooth, and Mitch had a tendency to use it to test his vehicle's acceleration. But today? Nope—not guilty.

He pulled over to the side and put the truck in park, grabbing registration papers as he waited for the RCMP to join him. The motion was getting far too familiar.

When he rolled down his window and discovered Nick Dowes with flashlight in hand, another curse escaped, only this one under his breath. This couldn't be good.

"Nick."

"Mitch." Nick cleared his throat. "Sorry about the unorthodox method of getting your attention, but I need to speak with you."

Fuck.

"No problem. Okay if I join you out there?" Because the last thing he needed was to be sitting in his truck like a schoolboy while being lectured by the man.

In answer, Nick stepped to the front of the vehicle. Mitch opened his door and followed him. Nick shifted uneasily in the headlight's beam, his breath escaping in puffs of white.

Mitch eased a hip against his truck bumper, ignoring the cold soaking through his jeans. "What's on your mind?" he asked.

Nick faced Mitch straight on. "This is awkward, and I've thought hard if I should even say anything, but in the end I feel it's only right for Anna's sake."

What the hell had gone down at the station today? Mitch chose his words with caution just in case this was about something else. "Are you warning me off dating her because you think you'd be better for her?"

Nick looked stunned for a second before blinking, a hint of amusement twisting his expression. "You think I'm jealous that you're seeing her? Oh, no. Anna's not my type."

The near lighthearted response was totally unexpected. Mitch's brain struggled to keep up, because now so much of Nick's behaviors made no sense. "If you're not angling to get together with her, then what's the issue?"

"I think you're a decent enough guy, and I figured since you are a decent guy, you'd like to know something. Chances are she's going to lose out on a big promotion because of you."

And with one statement, Nick knocked the wind from Mitch's sails. "Is she in trouble at work?"

Nick looked sheepish. "Someone messed up their filing, and I ended up with papers that weren't supposed to be on my desk. I think you're trustworthy enough, and you're smart enough to hear what I'm telling you. Anna's been shortlisted for a promotion, one that would push her up the ranks, and could possibly mean not only an advancement but a chance to head up her own division."

The wintery air seeped through Mitch's jacket. That had to be the reason his blood had gone cold. This wasn't about him and Anna, but about her getting to shine in a job he knew she loved. "Not a better job right here in Rocky, but headquartered somewhere else?"

Nick nodded. "We usually transfer fairly often as it is, although up to now Anna's remained stationed in Rocky for longer than most. She's far enough down the radar she's skipped being reassigned."

Mitch dragged a hand through his hair as he thought through this new revelation. The dilemma made his brain ache. Only he glanced at Nick with reservations. "Why are you telling me this? You don't even like me. You've been on my ass since before I started dating Anna."

"I don't dislike you. I think dating you makes Anna look bad, and that in turn makes our entire department look bad."

Jeez. "That's blunt."

The RCMP shrugged.

"When do you know more about the promotions?" Mitch asked.

Nick stared over Mitch's head. "The spring is when they'll make the announcements. For the next six months our commander is supposed to gather all kinds of information regarding her work, and her personal situations, and all of it gets sent off to the main office to be considered."

The implications were clear enough. Someone else would be making the decisions. Someone in an office far away, which meant the words on the page would be read as stated. There'd be no considering the situations, or the settings, if there were anything unusual listed like being caught in the middle of a wild Friday night party. Or that her boyfriend had been arrested under suspicion of grand theft auto. Or any of a number of crazy situations he'd led her into over the past months.

Nick hadn't mentioned anything specific regarding him and Anna's incident the previous night at Traders. Mitch hoped that meant no one knew, but the fact remained...

If Anna was going to make the promotion, she'd have to have a squeaky clean record. Her job that she'd worked so hard to achieve, and all the privileges it afforded her. The respect.

Mitch wanted to throw something. He wanted to use his fists, burn off the rising frustration.

He was trapped.

Nick glanced at him, concern etched onto his face. "You can't mention anything about the promotion. No one but you and I know, and the staff sergeant, of course."

Getting away from Nick to deal with this became more urgent by the minute. Mitch stood and nodded curtly. "Thanks for the info."

Nick patted Mitch's arm as he passed, pacing back to his cruiser.

Yet long after Nick had driven off Mitch still stood in the headlights of his truck at the side of the highway. The icy-cold December wind picked up, but he seemed unable to move, allowing the freezing gusts to stroke his cheeks, to tangle his hair.

His heart frozen as cold as the landscape around him.

Chapter Ten

SHE WENT to his house. Let herself in and waited for him to return.

They needed to figure out what came next, but the options seemed so limited. All she knew for sure was he'd made a difference in her life, and she wasn't about to bail on him. He'd proven he was more than a town bad boy, just like he'd said he would.

He deserved her respect for that. Respect, and maybe more.

The lights of his truck shone through the window, bouncing slightly as he drove the narrow approach and parked. Anna smoothed her sweater over her hips, nervously pacing to the front door to greet him. Stepping back before he could open the door so as not to be too needy.

The instant he was through the door she wanted to blurt everything out, but she held on. Waited until he stalked across the room and took her in his arms.

Somehow being held gave her hope. Anna slid his zipper down and buried her arms under his jacket, nestling in tight to his rock-solid chest and resting her cheek on him.

She found both warmth and comfort in the position. Maybe if she stayed like that for the next month, the nightmare hanging over her would vanish.

All too soon, though, Mitch kissed the top of her head and tugged himself free, stripping off his jacket and shoes and bringing her into the living room with him. He settled her close and kept her fingers in his hand. "What happened?"

Anna took a bracing breath. "I'm on report. Nothing official, but only because I was lucky. The staff sergeant said if I stay clean for a while, he'll remove all mention of my 'indiscretion' from the file."

His serious expression remained. "Nothing else? Nothing about us?"

She shook her head. The staff sergeant hadn't come out and told her not to see Mitch.

There were always going to be people who didn't like Mitch. Who would be suspicious of him, no matter what his actions proved. The decision she'd been struggling over was suddenly crystal clear. "We're okay," she insisted. "I know better than to act the fool in public. I just wasn't thinking."

He made a rude noise. "Our brains weren't the most active part at that particular moment, no." Mitch paused. "How long?"

"How long am I on report?" Anna shrugged. "He didn't say."

Mitch stared out the front window, his body stiff beside her. "I was so damn stupid, and the consequences could have been far worse."

"Hey, but they weren't." She stroked his fingers lightly. "I'll admit it, I was worried about my job, but you're worth it…" Confessing this much—she had to do it. "I'd risk it for you."

The golden flecks in his dark eyes seemed to fade. Mitch's answer came soft, nearly a whisper. "I don't want you to."

She stopped breathing. "Mitch?"

His entire body was so tight he looked ready to break. "Dammit, Anna, this changes everything. I like you. A lot. But I'm not worth you losing your job over, and I refuse to be the one to make that happen."

"I'm not losing my job." His surprising response toppled her confidence again. "We can just tone it down. Hell, it's not as if we can't fool around in private all we want."

He shook his head slowly, as if considering her words. "You're right. Contrary to how we've been acting, we're not teenagers. But we need to think this through hard."

Her soul dropped to her toes. "Mitch, you're the one who started this relationship. You're the one who said you wanted to be with me for more than sex. The past months have proved that I want to be with you as well. So…"

The next words stuck in her throat, though. What if she offered to take it to the next level, and he only wanted to stay at their current status?

"I did start this. And I think, and this is fucked up, but hear me out. I think we should stop seeing each other for a while."

Ice curled around her heart. "Because of my *job?*"

He snorted. "Because I can't keep my bloody hands off you in public, if you really want an excuse."

"Mitch, I was as much to blame as you were.'"

"So if the two of us can't control ourselves, that's all the more reason we should take a break for a while."

"A while?" Anna rocked back in her chair. "Stop seeing each other completely?"

Mitch shrugged. "I don't like it, but it's important you show your staff sergeant you're taking things seriously. Not much you can do that's more serious than this."

"Screw that," Anna snapped. "Why should we give up meeting in private? Fine if you want to take time off officially being together, but we've been together on the sly for months longer than anyone knew."

"You really think we could get away with it now? They'll be watching us like a hawk. We need a complete break." Mitch pulled his hands free from hers and stood, pacing away. "Think about it, Anna. You're in shit officially for the first time, but does the staff sergeant know about all the other places and times we've been caught. Or nearly caught?"

Anna prevaricated. "I don't know for sure."

Mitch stared her down. "Let the alarm die down. See how things go with work. Get that note taken off your file, and once you're in the clear, we can start seeing each other again."

"This is the stupidest thing." Anna joined him on the floor, fighting the sense of powerlessness that continued to rise.

"It is, and it's fucked up and I'm going to miss you like fucking crazy, but if it takes a few months to clear your name, I'm sure the hell not going to do anything to jeopardize your career. Don't make me—don't *let* me. I would hate myself forever."

"So I get no choice in the matter?" Anna demanded. "That's it? You've decided the best thing to do is we break up, and that's the end of the conversation?"

"Use your brain, not your libido, babe."

"What if I like using both?" Anna retorted. Only he had a point. She hated the circumstances intensely, but he was right. "So, what do we do? Make an announcement in the local paper? Stand on the street corner and shout it out?"

The scowl on his face was damn near frightening. "Fuck that. With all the gossips in this town, you mention at the gas station I was a jerk, and people will be all over the news like rabid cats."

Anna froze. "I'm not blaming you for anything. That's even stupider."

"It's not," Mitch insisted. "Someone's got to take the fall, and this time it should be me. We'll know the truth, and that's what's important. No matter what it looks like to everyone else. And eventually it won't matter shit."

"*If* we call it off, we say it's mutual, and that's final. I still don't like the idea in the first place."

"But you see the logic," Mitch noted. He stepped into her private space and caught her face in both his hands. "You worked hard to get to where you are today. If I have to stare at you from across the goddamn parking lot for a few months like some crazed stalker, then that's fucking fine with me. What's not fine is you doing something stupid that might screw up your career. I'm not worth that. No one is—so let's figure out the quickest and easiest way to let Rocky know we're done, then we move on."

Mitch leaned in and kissed her. Tender and soft at first, his lips stopping her from protesting any further. Then with increasing passion. Anna clung tighter as the kiss slowly heated.

If they were going to actually do this insane thing, she was taking the memory of his lovemaking with her. She slipped her hands to his shirt, rumbling in approval as he did the same, and they stripped each other. Lingering touches, tender caresses.

Anna stored away each moment as if preparing for a drought.

MITCH HAD been far too astute in his guess of how fast news would spread. She'd gone from the coffee shop to work, and in the five minutes it had taken to walk between the two locations, the welcome she got from Claire at the front desk made it clear the woman expected Anna to be upset, but wasn't sure if she should commiserate or give Anna a high five.

Her workmates might not have approved of Mitch, but they weren't going to cheer in her face that she'd called it off with him.

Nick said nothing. Well, not true. Nick said plenty, all about the inefficient way the station was dealing with its recycling and the lack of long-term vehicle-replacement plans. Anna tuned him out, grateful to be able to head to the high school for a couple hours in the afternoon, wandering the halls and being distracted by the angsty teenagers she'd grown surprisingly fond of.

Today she fit right in.

By the time Friday night rolled around, she couldn't take being stuck at home alone. Traders Pub and the regular Coleman family gathering beckoned. No way would she be dancing, but at least she'd have the company of the extended clan to divert her from her frustrations.

Anna joined the family on the bar side of the building. With all the cousins in the area, anywhere she went there was bound to be at least a few of them around. She settled into a chair by the pool tables next to her oldest brother Steve and examined the crowd.

She wondered if the numbness inside her was going to stick around the entire time she and Mitch worked this damn charade.

Steve stared at his beer and picked at the label, barely acknowledging her arrival. "Hey."

Anna was one step away from joining him in his gloomy attitude. "Where's everyone?" she asked while she waited for service.

Steve jerked his thumb over his shoulder. "Couple of the Six Pack boys are at the pool table with Trevor. I think there are more on the dance floor. The Whiskey Creek girls aren't here. They're having some kind of pre-baby wingding with Katy Thompson."

Right. She'd been invited, but didn't think hauling her pouty ass to a party for Mitch's sister was a good idea two days after they were supposed to have broken up.

Stupid, fucked-up world.

She tried to distract herself as she waited. "Where's Lee?" Her little brother was twenty-one and seemed determined to never miss any drinking opportunity. Between him and the youngest Coleman in the area, Rafe, Anna had been carefully turning a blind eye to their wild, but legal, antics.

Her question pulled a small shoulder shrug from Steve. "Dance floor? A group of giggling females swept in, and pulled him and Rafe over to the other side of the building."

"I bet the boys complained the entire time."

No answer. Steve stared into space.

"Are you even here tonight, Steve?" Anna prodded.

An enormous sigh escaped, and he finally glanced in her direction. "Sorry. Lots on my mind."

Her brother turned to watch the pool game, his melancholy expression slipping back in place.

Anna's discomfort grew as time passed. The lack of female cousins that night made it worse, and soon she felt as depressed as Steve looked, so she got up and wandered over to watch the pool game. The muttered comments and judgmental looks as people spotted her only added to the itch along her spine. She figured for the next few months she had this to look forward to every time she went out in public.

Damn Mitch for insisting they break up. Not only did she already miss him like crazy, she got to deal with stupid people and stupid assumptions.

The whispers going around were loud enough for her to overhear. Some said she'd dumped him. Some guessed Mitch had gotten tired of the straight-laced boring cop.

When someone suggested their relationship had all been a dare on his part, Anna gave up. She made her way back to her table to get her coat, evil fortune making her face the wrong direction at the right time to see Mitch pass through the doors from the dance-hall side of the bar.

Frustrating how her heart involuntarily sped up. How a knot formed in the back of her throat, and she was helpless to look away. She sank into the closest chair, mad at herself for wanting another glimpse.

He didn't even glance into the room. Just laughed loudly, a noisy crowd pressing around him. Regular customers at the pub stepped back warily as the newcomers strutted in as if they owned the place, loud joking and shouts carrying them forward. An edgy energy surrounded the group that seemed dangerous and borderline out of control. Everywhere Anna looked there were tattoos and metal and leather, the entire group poster children for one of Nick's profiling charts.

Yet when she tried looking at Mitch with critical eyes, all she saw was the man she'd come to respect, no matter how wild the trappings. A man she'd been willing to take a chance on.

They pulled tables together, the volume only rising as they settled into chairs. Mitch sprawled lazily, one arm stretched along the back of the chair next to him. The group seemed eager to give him attention.

Then the leather-clad blonde to Mitch's right dropped her arm around his shoulders. Anna's gut did a slow roll as the woman curled in tight, pressing close enough she could have checked his pulse without using her hands.

And that was one step farther than Anna could stomach.

Did she expect he'd spend time with others while they were taking a break? Of course. She hadn't taken it to the logical conclusion of him having to fend off feminine advances.

Anna jerked upright, dragging on her coat. Preparing to escape. Her rapid motion must have caught Mitch's attention, because his relaxed demeanor vanished, concern-filled eyes meeting hers. He peeled the woman off him, shot to his feet and headed for Anna's side.

So much for not making a public scene. She'd known they would run into each other in public sometime, but this was too soon and so not what she wanted.

"Anna, wait..."

She ignored Mitch's call, instead heading for the door. They couldn't do this here. Couldn't do anything that would make it better, because there *was* nothing that could make this better, not with what they'd decided. Anna shoved past chairs to get to the main aisle, not caring that she was all but fleeing the bar.

"You bastard."

A familiar voice—Steve's—rang out, followed by motion in her peripheral vision. Anna turned in time to see her brother grab Mitch by the shoulder, swinging him around. Steve's fist flew out in a rapid jab that Mitch did nothing to avoid. The blow struck his jaw, his head snapped back, and Mitch stumbled, attempting to stay on his feet.

"Stay away from her," Steve growled, moving forward with raised fists for another round. "You can't treat Anna like that, you ass."

"Steve, no." Oh damn, another thing she hadn't expected. Anna laid a hand on her brother's arm and tugged him back. "It's not worth it. Let it go."

"Anna, it's not what—" Mitch started again, but Steve rushed in, slamming his hands down on Mitch's chest. He fisted the front of Mitch's leather jacket, and who knows what he'd have done next except Anna shoved herself between them, facing her brother. Protecting Mitch. Awareness in every inch of her that he stood at her back, their bodies close enough if she leaned a tiny bit, she'd be in his arms.

She glared menacingly at her brother. "Drop it now, or I'll forget I'm off duty and haul your ass down to the station."

"But he—"

"I said drop it," Anna barked in her best cop voice.

She twirled to face Mitch, the tightness in her chest only increasing as she stared into his beautiful eyes. Those familiar yet now haunted eyes as his gaze darted over her face.

She wanted to throw all their plans into the garbage and wrap herself around him. Show all the naysayers watching that she thought he was worth so much that she'd...

She'd what? Possibly sacrifice her career? Mitch's words came back to her. *I'd hate myself if I ruined everything you've worked so hard for.*

It was a trap. One with no way out that didn't leave someone hurting. So instead of doing what her heart wanted, she pulled on every bit of acting ability she had.

Lifted her chin, and put her arms across her chest like a shield.

"Don't try to explain. Don't call me. Don't text. We're done, Mitch."

Anna focused on the exit, ignoring the faces around her. Steve was still at her side, and he shoved open the door, the freezing air numbing her lungs so they matched the rest of her.

"Anna, are you okay?"

She damn near sprinted toward her car. She needed to get away. Needed to be anywhere but here. "I'm fine."

He caught her arm and stopped her, and Anna lost it. There in the shadows of the parking lot, far enough away from the doors she couldn't be easily spotted, she broke down. Grabbed hold of her brother, pressed her face to his chest and let the tears escape.

They weren't a huggy family. Steve must have been thrown for a loop, but he tentatively wrapped his arms around her anyway. His awkward embrace was the only thing that kept her standing for the first minute. He patted her back and made soothing noises, and she pulled herself back together. The tear tracks on her cheeks froze when she gave him a final squeeze and stepped away.

A thick line furrowed Steve's brow. "Say the word, and I'll beat the shit out of him for you."

Oh God, what a disaster. She couldn't tell her brother the truth, but she couldn't stop her very real anguish from showing. Anna hiccupped as she fought for control and headed to her car. "Not a good idea. I'd hate to have to arrest you."

"Oh, Anna. I'm so sorry." Steve patted her arm again, his helplessness clear. "Not only for this crap, but for being an idiot myself. I should have paid more attention. Maybe I could have seen this coming."

"Not likely." Anna shook her head, unable to say anything more without choking up again.

"You didn't deserve that."

She slipped her key into her lock, needing to just go home. She kept her comment generic. "No one deserves to get dumped."

"I did."

Steve's blunt confession was enough to distract Anna from her misery. "What?"

"When Megan dumped me, I deserved it. I take people for granted," Steve admitted. "You, the folks. My ex."

Not much Anna could say in response, too overwhelmed by her personal pain.

Her brother clued in quick enough this time. "And I'm a shit for bringing that up now, other than to say I'll try to do better. You let me know if you need me, okay?"

Anna nodded, then escaped. A careful, deliberate escape, well under the speed limit. Instead of heading home, though, she drove in circles, not wanting to go back to a place filled with memories.

She was alone again, and this time it felt colder than before Mitch Thompson had twined his way into her life and her heart. She pulled to a stop under a tall light in the supermarket parking lot, hurting inside, and confused, and all she wanted was someone to hold her.

Not true. She wanted *Mitch* to hold her.

The cold air seeped in through the car doors, a fitting match for the ice in her heart. Anna rested her head back and closed her eyes.

Moving forward was her only option. She was strong, dammit. Strong enough to follow through with their plans. In the meantime maybe she could move forward into something even better than before.

This was a good thing, Mitch and her taking this break. She trusted him implicitly. Anna wiped the tears from her eyes and aimed her car home. She'd take it like a fresh start on life. Tomorrow she would begin some serious planning so that down the road she could have it all—her career and her wild man.

Tonight?

Tonight she was honest enough to admit she was going to crawl into bed and cry herself to sleep.

Chapter Eleven

MITCH KICKED his own ass over and over for that first, disastrous public meeting. Anna took the situation with a hell of a lot more grace than he would have. If she had turned up at Traders with another guy, he would have taken the asshole apart before tying her to his bedpost for a long hard discussion.

Anna? Other than that one moment when he thought she was going to slit his throat, she'd stuck to the plan.

Which sucked. Hugely.

Christmas passed. New Years. They followed their own rules and didn't contact each other on the sly. It felt as if he bumped into Anna a million times, though, yet never once did she look straight at him or acknowledge him. He was invisible, at least to her.

The reaction of the Coleman clan was mixed. As expected, word spread throughout her extended family that he and Anna had broken up. The good part most of the Colemans were decent enough to assume he hadn't done anything horrid. From them, there were no dire repercussions against him or the rest of his family. Katy's friends kept supporting her. The few times someone needed help with their cars, they still used the Thompson and Sons garage.

But anytime one of the Moonshine Coleman men crossed his path, Mitch remained extra wary and protected his balls. Steve and Trevor especially ended up being pains in his ass, which he understood since she was their little sister and all, but damn if their deliberate bullshit didn't rub him raw.

He fucking missed her like crazy.

The good part was the ache inside was getting familiar enough that if she got the promotion and moved away, he'd be used to the pain. He hated to think about it, but that possibility was real. Or if she decided at the end of it all that they weren't ever getting back together again, he'd already know how to live without his heart.

Mitch slipped out from the garage and walked to the tattoo shop on Main Street, the warming air a sure sign of approaching spring. So damn long since he'd been truly warm. He missed her fire, missed—

Jesus, he was doing it again. His thoughts drifted back to her even when he tried to avoid it.

The pain and pleasure he got from another tattoo couldn't compare to the pain he was living with. He'd let her go because it was the right thing to do, but no matter what happened he'd never forget her.

It was time to add another link to the chains he wore.

He pushed through the door of the shop, pulled off his coat and hung it up. The front desk was empty—Brad must be busy with another customer.

Mitch dropped into a chair to wait, thumbing through a bike magazine, unable to avoid hearing when voices rose from the back room.

"You like how it's turning out?" Brad asked.

"I do."

Mitch was on his feet and moving before he realized. That was Anna. What the hell?

"It looks awesome," Brad declared. "Ashley did a great job designing it."

"She did. But you're good, yourself. I like the shading you added."

Mitch had never wanted to bust down a door so bad in his life. Anna had gotten a tattoo? Fuck. He needed to see it more than he needed his next breath of air.

"Well, we're done for today. Take the usual precautions, let me know if you have any troubles. One more session will finish the shading."

Double fuck—Anna had a tattoo that had taken more than one session? Mitch's mind whirled with possibilities of where on her creamy skin she'd placed it.

Utter agony rolled through his soul that he'd missed being a part of her planning it. What if he never got to see it in living, breathing color?

He was still standing a few paces away from the door when she stepped out, her long hair loose and flowing instead of up in the ponytail she wore when she worked. He took in every detail about her hungrily while she was still distracted, talking over her shoulder to Brad.

Then she turned and jerked to a halt, the laughter in her eyes fading to longing. "Mitch."

He had to wet his lips before he could speak. "Anna. You're looking good."

"Thanks."

Nothing more. Safe. Public.

He kept staring, soaking in every detail. "Ashley drew you a tattoo, did she?"

Her eyes widened, and her cheeks flushed. Involuntarily, images from their night spent with Ashley and Cassidy raced through his brain, and damn if his cock didn't react.

Anna straightened slightly, her gaze locked on his so there was no possible way he could miss the heartfelt intensity with which she delivered the words. "It's something I decided I wanted," she said softly. "Life's too short to put off things that are important."

There was nothing he could say in response, because he didn't want her holding back and waiting for him. But the truth tore him apart. She was what was important to him, and he wanted her right now. Every bloody second of the day.

She stepped around him, her fingers brushing him with the faintest of a caress as she headed for the coat rack.

Had the contact been deliberate? He ached to catch her in his arms to tell her he was sorry for all the things they'd missed doing together. That he wanted to take it back about breaking up being the best thing for them. He wanted to share that more than anything he wished he could be with her, and be good for her.

But he couldn't. He couldn't be any of those things, not for certain, so he did the only thing he could.

He let her walk away.

IT HAD been a long winter full of lessons Anna hadn't really wanted to learn. Yet, no matter how trite it was, as spring approached hope stirred in her heart.

She missed Mitch, jackass of the century that he was. He'd taught her things while they'd been together. About living life to the fullest and not worrying about others' responses.

The time apart had taught her that she was stronger than she thought.

Maybe it was pathetic, but she often found herself smoothing the paper she still had from him, the one with the date-like things he'd said he wanted to do with her. She missed that man. Missed the strangely earnest hoodlum who had shared his heart with her during their quiet moments together.

"Constable Coleman. Can I see you in my office?"

She was on her feet, swaying as she considered why the staff sergeant was calling her. "I'll be right there."

Her commanding officer put her out of misery immediately after she'd closed the door behind her. "I thought you might like to witness this."

He slipped a page from the file on his desk and ran it through the paper shredder.

Anna took a deep, deep breath, the extra oxygen making her lightheaded. "Thank you, sir."

Max nodded. "I have zero complaints about your work, and there have been no further incidents, so we'll put it all behind us." He paused. "I will admit I was surprised to hear that you and Mitch were no longer seeing each other at all."

Well, that was an unexpected turn in the discussion. "We thought it best."

Her commanding officer pulled another page from her file and stared at it. "I think I should tell you about this. It's a letter of reference of a sort. I got it in the mail back in December, and it's a glowing report of your skills as an officer."

"Always good to know people appreciate our work." Anna waited to be dismissed, but Max obviously had more on his mind.

He read a few lines. "'An asset to the force, and a strong member of the community.' You have quite the admirer." His gaze traveled farther down the page. "He goes on at length regarding your skills, but what I'm still confused about is this section. 'I'm completely to blame for any recent black marks against her record, and hope that you will take that into consideration as she is considered for promotion.'"

Oh God. "Mitch Thompson wrote that."

Max nodded. "Seems to think a lot about you. Was totally willing to throw himself under the bus to get you off the hook, although we both know he's wrong in that. He's not to blame for anyone else's behavior."

"Of course he's not. I take full responsibility for myself."

"And that's why I've cleared your slate. Your actions have proved your value to this department." Max frowned. "Although I admire his guts in sending this to me, I have no idea where he got the idea you were up for promotion. Nick is the only one who put in for job advancement last fall."

Anna's brain felt filled with puzzle pieces trying to fit together correctly. "Nick's up for a promotion?"

Staff Sergeant Max put a finger to his lips. "They're still in the works. We're in the final months. I'll be asking

133

for feedback from you later this week, in fact, as one of his closest coworkers."

Nick was up for promotion, and Mitch knew about promotions back in December? Anna shook herself back to alertness to answer her commanding officer. "Whenever you'd like to talk, let me know."

"And Anna—I want to make this clear. I have no issues with you seeing anyone in town that you want. My only expectation is that your behavior in public remain exemplary."

A shimmer of light broke through the mental haze. She smiled at him. "Thank you for that, sir."

"Thank you for proving me right in your skills." He slipped the note from Mitch back in her file. "I have a feeling there's someone else who will be pleased to hear your news."

A strange mix of euphoria and confusion floated her back to her office. Sheer relief was the highest emotion followed by a nagging tic at the back of her brain. Why had Mitch thought she was up for promotion? Had she ever said anything to make him think that?

It was one thing she would definitely ask when she contacted him with her good news. Part of her wanted to call him that very minute, but if the past five months had taught her anything, though, it was patience. She'd wait for that evening and the privacy of her own apartment.

Nick stuck his head in the office door. "You have the final reports on the last break-in?"

Anna paused, adjusting her brain to focus on work again. "I'm pretty sure I put them on your desk."

Her partner stepped in and flipped through the pile. "Got any plans after the picnic is over this weekend?"

"Nothing unusual." Anna wasn't about to tell him she was planning to hold a private party with Mitch to celebrate that pile of shredded paper in the staff sergeant's garbage bin. "You? Talk to anyone interesting out there today?"

"Pulled Mitch Thompson over. Well, a whole gang of riders, including Mitch."

Hearing his name mentioned so soon after thinking about him made her smile, but she focused on staying nonspecific until they were officially back together. "So the bikers are out again, are they? With the great weather, I figured they'd be on the road soon."

"That guy, I swear." Nick shook his head. "One minute I think there's a rational person under all that ink, and the next he proves he's nothing more than brawn and attitude."

Anna held her tongue.

"He's obviously not stupid—he does listen to reason occasionally, but you should have heard the garbage he spilled at me today. Should have known one moment of sanity doesn't make a man sane."

Something about Nick's comments didn't sit right, especially not when mixed with the staff sergeant's information. Anna turned slowly, trying to make sense of her forebodings. "Nick, when else have you talked to Mitch? Other than while pulling him over?"

He stiffened, eyes widening, and an awkward pause went on and on until she interrupted it. She might be leaping to conclusions, but something in her gut told her she was right. Mitch mentioning promotions. Nick being the one up for one.

"Did you say something to Mitch about me?" She felt her anger stirring. While she and Mitch had discussed the best way to deal with her reprimand, this sounded as if something else had gone down without her knowledge.

Nick walked around her and closed the door to their office. "I didn't...exactly. I might have encouraged him to think of your future with the department and—"

Oh my God, her guess was correct. "So you butted into my life? You had no right."

"You were making us look bad," Nick snapped, colour flushing his cheeks. "Maybe you want to stay at your current level of near-incompetence, but I have aspirations to do a lot more and—"

Anna shot up a hand to cut him off again, utter fury creating a black hole in her belly. "Near *incompetence*? You want to explain that one to me? I have a perfect record with the department, including being involved in liaison work and high-risk security details."

"You only got the liaison position because you're a woman." Nick's control vanished, and his words came out a shout.

Her rage bloomed so quickly it had already passed being an inferno. Instead, her fury was blue hot, like a core of dry ice burning from the intensity of her frozen emotions. She ground out her words, soft and low. "If you have such a low opinion of my skills, why did you not decline when you were offered me as a partner?"

Nick wouldn't meet her eyes.

Another thought whispered through, shock registering as revelation kicked in. Some of the pain she and Mitch had suffered through was because Nick had an agenda. *Nick* was the one looking for things.

"You asked to be my partner, didn't you?"

He headed toward his desk. "Maybe we should put this aside for another day when we've cooled off."

"Bull fucking shit on that," Anna spat out. "You asked to partner with me in the hopes of getting some weird glory from being with the lone woman on active duty, didn't you? What is your game, Nick?"

"I'm up for promotion, okay? Is that what you want to know?" Nick slammed himself down in his chair. "It's my chance to get out of town and move to a position with some political clout."

"This...was all about you getting ahead."

"Of course. Like any intelligent person, I'm doing what I can to make sure my career advances in the right direction."

Anna's nails were digging holes in her palms. "By running roughshod over anything or anyone in your way? Oh, you've got all the makings of a great politician, I can tell already."

Nick narrowed his eyes. "Getting involved with Mitch was a stupid move for your career, and there's no way even you didn't know it."

Ice flooded her veins. "Even *me*? As in 'Anna Coleman who isn't that smart' or is this some kind of 'you're a woman, and you should get your ass back in the kitchen' comment? I'd suggest you consider real hard before you answer if you don't want to find out exactly how well I learned self-defense during training."

Revelation struck. This was why Mitch had insisted they break up. He'd fallen for whatever lies Nick had told him. Mitch had gone and done what he thought best— calling them off—without telling her why. Yes, she'd agreed in the end, but still...

It would take a little more time to work through exactly how she wanted to deal with him.

Right now, Nick was front and center on her shit list.

Her partner continued to prove he wasn't very smart. He wasn't shutting up. "The Thompsons aren't the kind of—"

She'd had more than enough of his bull. "No more, Nick. Don't even try to dig yourself out of this hole. From now on you will keep your nose out of my business and out of the Thompsons' business, you understand? You don't go near them. You don't try to find things to mess up their lives. Consider them your own private kryptonite, or I will report every single thing you did, and not only will your current political aspirations die, but your career will be over."

Actual fear shone in his eyes, as if Nick had finally realized he'd gone too far. "What are you going to do?"

"I need time to think, but my personal life is none of your goddamn business. I've told you that before, but if that's not absolutely crystal clear this time around, we have a major problem."

Nick nodded, then backed off. "The reports are supposed to go through in the next month."

"Reports?" She wasn't giving an inch. Staff Sergeant Max had already told her this, but making Nick squirm was as necessary as breathing.

He turned white, but continued. "Promotion reports. I'm up for one. I…told Mitch you were the one being considered."

She had nothing left inside to burn as the final confirmation of her suspicions was revealed. "Then you'd better hope that for the next month I don't get sick of seeing your face. Get out of here."

Nick shot from the room as if jet propelled.

Anna sat in silence and tried to recalibrate her life. Her career was back within the safety zone. But her career wasn't enough.

It appeared Mitch had planned to end them for her own good before they'd even spoken. Even more, he'd made the temporary break-up about him not being able to keep his hands off her instead of telling her about the potential promotion. He'd taken control of the situation instead of working as a team.

No matter that he'd had good intentions, he didn't get to make those kind of life-altering decisions without her, and the sooner he came to understand that, the happier they would be going into the future.

The future. They had one, and she was looking forward to it with everything in her.

Once Mitch Thompson had finished the crap-ton of explaining and apologizing he had ahead of him.

Chapter Twelve

MITCH ZIGGED instead of zagging, turning away from the large tents that had been set up in the community fairgrounds. The three days of May fair were usually a time for kicking back and relaxing.

Forget relaxing and enjoying himself—the numbness inside refused to go away. And while he'd promised his family he'd come to the grounds for a while, he was getting tired of having to duck around corners to avoid getting beat on by surly Coleman males.

The first time Steve and Trevor tracked him down Mitch had taken the punishment. After that, he wasn't about to simply stand there and let them knock him around, but he figured hurting any of Anna's kin also wasn't on the agenda. Thus the ducking and hiding, and didn't that chafe his ass in a whole new way.

Mitch glanced back at his sister and her boyfriend without really seeing them. While he was glad things seemed to be working out for her, his world remained in limbo.

Every day he and Anna were apart, it seemed more likely they were never going to be together again. He cussed his fucked-up life.

He slowed his pace and wandered aimlessly past the coffee tent. He didn't want to go into the animal yard, didn't want to head back to the main fairgrounds where the crowds were gathering for the arcade games and beer tents.

His feet took him toward the parking lot, and he eyed his bike, debating if he should simply go home. At the moment the last thing on his mind was partying.

He'd left his ride at the opposite side of the lot, and the farther from the fairgrounds, the more peaceful the air became. The quiet song of spring birds escaped from the branches, and Mitch stepped into the cool shade cast by the trees to breathe deeply.

The next second he was on the ground, his hands twisted behind him, the knee strategically pressed into his upper back rendering him immobile.

"Fuck." The Colemans had caught up with him again. "Didn't you get enough of my blood on your hands the last time?" Mitch demanded, struggling to break free.

"Not yet, but I'm considering it really hard."

His brain clicked into gear the same moment cold metal clicked around his wrists.

"Anna?" He twisted his head, cursing the pain that shot through him that made him freeze in position even as hope rose. "Goddamn it, what the hell are you doing?"

"I'll ask the questions. When I'm ready." She let his handcuffed wrists go, a firm hand grasping his cheek as she rearranged herself over his body. Whatever training she'd had, Mitch couldn't believe how tightly she had him controlled. The excruciating jolt of pain that struck when he tensed to buck her off encouraged him to lie very, *very* still.

"Am I under arrest for something?" He wriggled his wrists, shaking the cuffs. "What is going on?"

"I have three questions. You get three responses. Don't waste them," Anna suggested. "Number one. When you insisted we needed to temporarily call our relationship off, were you basing your decision on a discussion with Nick?"

Oh hell. Mitch scrambled to find an answer that wouldn't get his balls busted. "It wasn't like that—*ow*. Dammit, *stop it.*"

The instant he'd spoken she'd increased the pressure pinning him in place.

Anna ignored his complaint, just settled harder over him. "Two more tries. Did you really throw away all that time we'd spent together because you had some egotistical male idea you knew what was *best* for me?"

"Jesus, Anna, let me explain—"

She didn't move. Mitch breathed slowly through his nose before opening his mouth and letting the words escape.

"I'm sorry. God, you can't know how fucking sorry I am."

The weight on his back diminished, even though she kept a tight hold on his neck. Mitch waited until she knelt beside him, her eyes meeting his for the first time in forever, and the pain that had built over the past five months exploded.

"I didn't want to risk fucking up your job any further. When Nick told me you had a chance for a promotion—"

"Nick lied."

Her sharply spoken comment made him recoil as if a knife blow had been aimed at his gut. "*What?*"

"Nick's the one up for promotion. He thought me being associated with you was putting a blemish on his shine, so he lied to you." She shoved a hand against Mitch's chest and rolled him halfway to his back. "And you damn well believed him."

Black anger rolled through Mitch, blurring his vision. "I'm going to kill him."

"Get in line," Anna snapped. "But this isn't about him. It's about you, and that you made a decision about my life without so much as blinking. *Damn you*, Mitch. No matter how wrong Nick was, you were just as bad. You were a bastard."

Words poured out of him.

"The hell I didn't blink." Mitch struggled to a sitting position, his arms still trapped behind him. "I missed you so much. Every time I thought about you, it was like I was cutting myself in two. I couldn't sleep. Every time I closed my eyes, you were all I saw. That damn reprimand had to be erased, and if you were up for a career promotion, I wasn't about to ruin your chances. Breaking up with you was the only thing I could think of."

"Fine. So here's a different question for you. We agreed to break up. We said nothing about you walking away from me and straight into another woman's arms." Her eyes flashed at him, the pale blue burning him like dry ice. "You found another woman in less than forty-eight hours and shoved her under my nose? Did you even know her name before you fucked her?"

"I didn't fuck her. It wasn't like that."

"You looked damn cozy that night at Traders."

Mitch broke. "I haven't been with anyone since you," he roared. "And if anything, her twin was the one I had to worry about. Damn guy has grabby hands like no one I've ever met before."

Her expression went blank with shock. "Really?"

"I'm organizing a toys-for-tots bike rally with that group, which is crazy like hell, but I'm serious. That's all we were doing that night."

Anna didn't speak, but she looked far more willing to listen.

"There's been no one but you. No one, because there was no one I wanted more than you." Mitch leaned over so he could stare into her eyes, the intensity of what was inside pouring out with his words. "Every time I wake up, I smell the scent of your shampoo and it makes me hard, and then I remember that you aren't there anymore, and it's my fault. It's like you're in my veins, dammit. Everywhere I look I see things that remind me of you. Every song I hear. It drives me crazy, and yet the reminders are the only things keeping me sane. There were no other women, Anna. Since I couldn't have you, I didn't want anyone else."

Her face was still drawn and tight, but her eyes were far more alive than he'd seen in months. Hope stirred inside—the faintest hint. No matter how stupid he felt at being played by Nick, there was a light ahead of them, and he reached for it with everything he had.

"I was wrong, Anna. I should have talked to you, because my great decision caused us both nothing but pain. I've missed you so fucking much. I've missed your passion and your fire, and your soft side and your sexy smile. Damn, I've missed everything about you." He reached for her, forgetting momentarily about the handcuffs, his arms jerking to a stop before he could take her back in his arms where she belonged. "Do we need the cuffs anymore?"

Anna raised a single brow. "You don't think you're done apologizing, do you?"

"Hell no, but I can apologize a lot better with my hands free."

A reluctant snort escaped her. "I bet you could."

She glanced over her shoulder and reached for his wrists, but instead of letting him go, she helped him to his feet and tugged him toward the parking lot.

"Anna?"

"Trust me."

Mitch stepped quickly at her side. He deserved whatever hell she put him through for falling for Nick's lies. He was going to fucking get revenge on the man no matter what, though.

The only good thing seemed to be that the months of pain were over. "I'm sorry," he repeated.

"You'd better get used to saying that." Anna paused beside a transport trailer, guiding him to the front sleeping quarters. "You have five full months of *I'm sorry* to catch up on."

"As long as it takes," Mitch vowed. "Whatever it takes."

She jerked the door open and gestured him into the small space.

Mitch glanced around, shuffling his feet on the tiny floor area. "Whose trailer is this?"

"Steve's. Trevor and Steve brought animals for the petting zoo, and the trailer is the biggest we own."

She planted a hand between his shoulders and pushed him toward the corner where a straight-back chair was tucked into the compact space. Mitch jiggled the cuffs again.

"Forget it. Sit down," Anna ordered.

He turned and obeyed, impatience and worry he'd pushed too far, too fast warring inside. "So…"

Anna pulled the elastic from her hair, carefully laying it on the table to the right of the twin-sized mattress. "So, you wait. I'm in uniform, and while I've got plans, they don't involve being kicked off the force for inappropriate behavior. I don't go on shift for another fifty minutes."

Mitch's mouth went dry as her hands went to the top buttons of her khaki-brown shirt. "You're going to torture me, right? As punishment for being an ass."

The top curves of her breasts appeared. Absolute torture, whether she intended it or not. His body tightened as if he'd been on a tight leash and aching for her for months—all true.

The fabric opened, falling aside to reveal flashes of smooth skin and one of her flaming-red bras.

"Sweet Jesus, woman."

Anna's fingers slipped lower to her belt and zipper, pulling the leather open, sliding the metal down. "Five months thinking about what I wanted to do with my life, Mitch. Part of me wants to thank you, because as much as it sucked, it forced me to make some decisions. I've changed in that time."

"And part of you wants to take a very small knife and skin me slowly?"

"Then sprinkle you with salt. Yeah, that about sums it up." Anna pushed her pants to the floor and stepped out of them.

When had she taken off her boots? Mitch must have missed it while fixated on the tiny red patch of fabric covering her mound. "Tell me you forgive me. Tell me you still want me." He'd beg if he had to. Anything to keep her there with him, not just in the trailer stripping off her clothes, but there in his life.

Anna lifted her chin. "I forgave you last night after I tossed a few darts at your picture. Doesn't mean I'm not still pissed. You don't make decisions about my life without me, Mitch. Being without you broke my heart. "

"And mine as well. So take these damn cuffs off me so I can pick up the pieces and start putting them back together again."

She held out a hand to ward him off, even though he was the one restrained. "First we need to get one thing straight. We're here having this conversation because I choose to focus on the fact you made a wrong decision for the right reasons. But if you go around me again, Mitch Thompson, I will use those cuffs on another part of your anatomy and you will sing soprano for the rest of your earthly days."

Mitch could work with that, only... "Don't try to tell me not to protect you."

"I don't need protecting, I need a partner who wants me, all of me." Her eyes flashed. "Which reminds me—no killing Nick."

A growl escaped before he could stop it. "Fine, then I'll just maim him a little."

"No, you will leave him alone. I'm dealing with him in a work-appropriate manner, and you will not go and screw up everything I've put into place."

"I don't know that I can do that." Mitch shook his head. "The bastard lied to us. What the fuck are you defending him for?"

"He'll get his own in a short enough time," Anna promised. "But if you get yourself arrested for beating the crap out of him, I swear I'll leave you in jail to rot, and there will be no coming back. Ever."

He listened to what she was saying, but Nick getting off scot-free burned. "A little retribution is in order."

"I'd prefer to put him out of my head and deal with other more pressing issues." Anna stepped into his personal space, naked limbs and open shirt turning the conversation to a whole new topic. "I'm in charge. Say it, Mitch."

"Anything," he vowed. "Anything you want."

She pulled a condom from her shirt pocket, and a million dirty urges rushed along his spine along with unbelievable joy. "You haven't been with anyone else?" she asked.

He shook his head. "Only you, ever since we got tested back in the fall."

Anna dropped the package on the table, then turned him to face the wall, his palms bumping her belly as she unlocked the cuffs. "You know what I want? I want you."

Her words became the key that set him free. He twirled and before the cuffs hit the floor with a resounding clang, he had her lifted in the air. Anna wrapped her arms around him, and he took the single step needed to drop them to the mattress, reaching for a kiss with a desperate hunger.

She wanted him? He was never letting her go again.

ANNA'S HEART raced, but all thoughts of her job and Nick and his lies and their past hurt slipped away as Mitch joined their lips. His long, hard body pressed her to the mattress, but all she could focus on at first was the devastation of him kissing her senseless. Teeth and tongue, breaths mingling until the distance between them faded to a memory, and she knew this was where they both belonged.

Together. United. Frantically touching as if their lives depended on the next caress. The next connection of fingers over skin.

Mitch kissed his way to her throat, sucking lightly as he pushed a hand under her bra, palm resting over her breast. "I ached for you," he whispered. "Every night I was tempted to drive to your house and beg for you to let me come in. Beg on my hands and knees for you to forget everything I'd said about it being better for us to be apart."

Anna curled her fingers through his hair, her throat gone tight at the emotion in his voice. Her tough, bloodthirsty biker was ripping her apart with his sweet words because they were true. So very true—and clear in his every touch. "I probably would have pointed a shot gun at you at first," she confessed. "After that night at the bar."

He pulled back and stared into her eyes. "You already shot me in the heart."

The final knot of anger and pain melted. "Take off your clothes," she whispered.

Mitch's eyes widened as his gaze traveled down the skin exposed by her open shirt. "Your tattoo. Sweet fuck, I need to see it."

"Clothes off first." Anna sat back, clutching the front of her shirt together.

Mitch toed off his boots, grabbed the back of his shirt and whipped it over his head. Anna watched eagerly as he stripped, hard muscles and ink coming back into view. She loved the curving line along his hips, the chains shifting on his torso. Loved the way his biceps flexed as he moved, making the flames come alive.

Burning upward, like the coldness inside her was melting. "You're so beautiful."

He grinned as he sat back on the edge of the mattress. "Guys aren't beautiful, and I'm the least beautiful of them all. I'm rough and dirty, and far too stupid for you." His dark gaze caught hers again as he prowled closer. "Which means I'm too stupid to know you should kick my ass out forever. You're stuck with me, Anna. I'm never letting you go again."

"We make decisions together, Mitch Thompson," she reminded him.

"Then decide to get naked, Anna. I've been going fucking nuts wondering what you got marked with."

They were in tight quarters in the front of the trailer, but having him crowd her was right. They didn't need much room when all they wanted was to get as close as humanly possible.

Mitch pushed the fabric off one shoulder, fixated on her torso as the bold lines of her tattoo came into sight. "Hello, gorgeous. *Jesus*, Anna. That's damn hot."

He brought her to her knees, tugged the shirt away and tossed it to the floor, her bra following a second later. The entire time his gaze stroked her skin as he admired her tattoo.

"I loved your flames," Anna admitted. "But I wanted my own. Something that was uniquely me—and Ashley designed it. I can wear a swimsuit, and nothing shows."

Mitch frowned. "You want to hide this? That's criminal."

"I thought about it a lot, Mitch. I have a lot of things I'm passionate about, but I really don't mind also having a private side." Anna caught his chin in her fingers, stroking the rough shadow on his jaw. Goose bumps rose over her skin. "It's not that I'm hiding who I am, but I only want to share that part of me with certain people. I don't need to let it all out all the time as long as I can be completely myself with people I trust."

She waited, needed him to understand this. Needing this final step to register—

Her heart couldn't take it if he didn't accept her completely, as she was. She knew what she wanted, but could he give her all of what she needed? Her heart's desire?

Mitch trailed a finger over the flames that started at her collarbone. A thin line that followed down under where her bra strap would go before curling around the outside of her breast. Flames licked under the curve before edging down her waist and across her bikini area. The marks stopped just shy of her sex, and he lingered there, flipping his hand over and gently cupping her mound.

Slowly his head rose, his eyes meeting hers. "You can keep your fire hidden from everyone else, as long as you promise to always let it burn with me."

The final tumbler clicked into place. Anna leaned into him and kissed him fiercely. Taking back what had been stolen from them.

Maybe Mitch had gone about it wrong, but it would be stupid to keep punishing them both for Nick's crimes. This was where they belonged. This was what she needed.

The warmth of his palm heated her as he pressed one finger through her folds. At the same time he stroked her clit softly, he slipped his tongue into her mouth and deepened the kiss. Easing her back to the mattress and taking control from her.

He played her body like he knew everywhere she needed to be touched. His lips on her neck, on the upper curve of her breast. Tongue tracing the tattooed flames then sneaking over so he could wrap his lips around her nipple and suck.

"I thought you would ravish me," Anna confessed, running her fingers through his hair again and again as he moved from one breast to the other until she was breathless.

"I want to savour you. I want to taste every inch of you until you're mine all over again." He kissed the small dot of flame Ashley had designed to shoot toward her belly button, then lifted his gaze. His pupils had widened, the dark-as-coal centers blending into the dark of his irises until she couldn't see anything but his desire for her. He paused. Swallowed hard. "I want to make love to you, Anna."

Oh *God*. Nothing left to hurt. Nothing but his touch taking her to paradise far too quickly. He snatched up the condom she'd dropped on the table, but she stilled his hand. "You don't need it. I haven't been with anyone since you, either."

His eyes flashed, and he was back, cock nudging between her folds. Gold piercing rubbing just right. Familiar. Brand new. Slowly filling her body.

Filling her soul.

He didn't look away once, his fingers linked through hers, pinning her hands to the mattress on either side of her head. One slow rock after another he joined them together. One thrust, then again, deeper still as she lifted her legs and locked her ankles around his back.

Mitch kissed her, tender and oh-so-perfect as the tension in her mind and body changed completely to sexual need. Anna squeezed his fingers tight, blinking back the moisture as he bumped his pelvis against her clit to make her come.

"Mitch..."

Deeper, not just a physical connection. Not just their bodies. Mitch whispered the words. "I love you, Anna."

She fought to be able to answer him. To do anything, but she was too busy accepting the wave of pleasure that swamped her. Shaking as she stared into his eyes and watched him find release as well.

He settled slightly to one side, kissing her face, clutching her close. Rolling them in the small space and draping her over his body.

It was crazy, but it was right.

"I love you too, Mitch." Anna breathed against his chest as he stroked her hair. Contentment and peace blanketed them.

There was a noise at the trailer door an instant before it swung open. Anna shot to a sitting position, snatching up the bed sheet they'd shoved aside earlier. Mitch twisted upright as well, his arm going around her protectively.

Steve's eyes widened for a moment before he grimaced and averted his gaze. "Anna? What the fuck is going on?"

"Have you never heard of knocking?" Anna demanded.

"It's my damn trailer. Why the hell should..." Steve paused. "Wait. Stop trying to distract me. What is *he* doing here?"

Mitch's low laugh teased up Anna's spine, and she had to fight to keep from giggling.

"Nothing you need to worry about," Anna insisted. "Mitch and I were just having a...discussion about... About..." She fought for something to say that wasn't dirty. Because, dear Lord, her brother was standing in the damn doorway, and she and Mitch were both buck-naked.

"Carburetors," Mitch offered.

A snort escaped before she pulled it together.

Steve growled. "In the nude? I swear, Thompson, if you're playing hard and fast with my sister, you're a dead man walking."

"I promise I have only the utmost respect for your sister. Now get your ass the hell out of here," Mitch ordered. "You want to discuss this with me later, fine."

"No," Anna snapped. "There will be no discussions. Steve, Mitch and I are dating. He'll be joining us at the family dinner on Sunday. So, no more threats, no more trying to jump him in dark alleys. Get over it, and get out."

The door slammed shut, and Anna collapsed back on the bed, peals of laughter escaping her. Mitch joined in, his deep rumble washing over her and melting the final frozen bits inside.

"You're still not done apologizing," she warned once she could speak again.

"Hell no, I'm not." Mitch turned his head to the side so his cocky grin was front and center. "But I can apologize much better once we find some rope."

Laughter bubbled up again, and it felt so good to be set free from the cage she'd been trapped in. All the hurt seemed so far away, as if the past was fading rapidly and only the future mattered.

The future.

It was going to take some delicate juggling to keep Nick alive long enough to get what was coming to him.

She propped herself up on Mitch's chest, fingers of her right hand still linked with his as he stroked her naked back with the other. "So, here's what's going to happen over the next two months..."

Epilogue

FAMILY DINNERS had changed.

Well, some things had changed. Mitch ducked the leftover bun his youngest brother Troy threw at his head. A soft cry rang from the back room, and Katy half rose to her feet before her fiancé gestured her down.

"I'll grab the kiddo. Finish your dessert." Gage winked at Mitch. "Unless any of the uncles in the room want to do diaper duty."

Four grown adults found ways to make themselves look busy as Gage laughed and left.

Mitch's dad leaned back in his chair and sighed happily. "Damn good meal, Katy. Thank you."

His sister shook her head. "Not me. Mitch and Anna made the lasagna."

His dad's eyes widened. "Well, now. Good job. But where is the prettiest cop in all of Clearwater County? Doesn't seem fair she's feeding us, but missing dinner."

Mitch checked his watch. "She should be off shift soon. She'll be here shortly."

Keith nodded, then turned to his oldest son and started quizzing him on the work plans for the next day. Clay, Len and Troy all got into it with him, arguing about whether it was worth purchasing some new diagnostic tool or not.

Mitch didn't bother listening very hard, more interested in looking out the window to spot Anna as soon as she arrived. He had plans, but they were going to be tough to follow through on if she had to bail for work.

But then, they would have tomorrow. And the tomorrow after that. Mitch held his secret and tried not to gloat so hard someone in the family noticed.

"You two are good together."

He turned to face his sister. Katy had lifted her feet to her chair and wrapped her arms around her shins, smiling at him. The shadows under her eyes were no longer from stress or fear, but from a healthy baby waking her up at night.

"Anna?"

Katy nodded. "I like her. She was pretty amazing the times I had to deal with her over the past year. Smart, yet kind." Katy paused briefly before grinning harder. "She's just about everything I've ever wished for in a sister."

Mitch eased his chair back. "Not that you're trying to push any kind of agenda on me, right?"

"Me be bossy? Nah. Never." Katy uncurled herself and picked up plates from the table, whistling shrilly as she moved to the sink. "Hey, guys. I'll clear, but someone else is washing. Heads up."

"You tell 'em, girl." Anna slipped through the back door, standing in the entranceway with a happy smile on her face. "Hey, Mitch."

He was at her side in a second flat. It was so strange and yet so right to have her there in the middle of his family. The past months had changed a lot of things, and this was one of the best parts. "You hungry? I saved you a piece."

"You're such a liar," Katy cut in. "*I* saved you a piece from the rampaging horde."

Anna laughed. "I'm good. We had celebratory cake at the station, so I'm full for now." She grabbed Mitch's hand. "Can I steal you away from dish-duty? Got something to show you."

"No problem by me."

She waved at his brothers and dad, and answered their questions while Mitch dragged on his coat.

"Drop by the shop tomorrow," Keith ordered. "Stop by for coffee."

"I'll do that," Anna promised.

Mitch followed her outside, delighted to find she had her new bike with her, the one that he'd helped her buy. "Are we riding?"

"Maybe later. First take me back to the station."

What the heck was going on?

Only, if there was one thing he'd learned over the past month, arguing with Anna wasn't worth it. Besides, it was far more fun to simply go along for the ride. "Sure."

He pulled on his helmet then mounted, loving the moment when she crawled behind him and leaned in tight, her strong arms sliding around his body. The trip to the station was far too short to enjoy having her intimately pinned against him.

"We need to do a long road trip," Mitch teased as he pulled into the staff parking lot.

"You tell me when you can get time off, and I'll organize my holidays." Anna tugged him to the side. "Look."

For a moment he didn't see what she was showing him. A couple of RCMP cruisers sat waiting, but the stall in front of him was empty. Then he spotted it. There attached to the wall. *Reserved parking for Corporal Anna Coleman.* "Hello, really?"

Anna touched the nameplate on the wall then turned to face him, an ear-to-ear grin shining out. "The Staff Sergeant gave it to me this afternoon and had the maintenance team put it in place right away. Wait until I tell the kids at the high school—they're going to be thrilled."

"This means you got a promotion?" Mitch picked her up and twirled her in the air, listening to her laughter ring over them. He lowered her to the ground and cupped her shining face in his hands. "Hot damn. Congrats, babe. I had no idea you were in line for one."

She touched her fingers over his, her delight rushing like a waterfall. "Well, it seems there's this opening on the staff roster they needed to fill."

Mitch checked the parking lot to make sure they were alone. "Tell me Nick got his ass fired for being a shit."

Anna shook her head, still smiling. "Oh, no. That's why we were having cake. He got his promotion."

"Ah, *fuck.*"

"It's good. Trust me." Anna's obvious happiness made no sense, but before he could demand an explanation, she held out a hand to him. "Come on, let's go for a ride."

She refused to tell him more. At least until he'd taken them into the mountains, following the descending sun until he could pull off by the side of a tiny lake. Mitch parked, then picked her up, ignoring her laughing protests as he carried her to where there was a picnic table overlooking the lake and the mountain view. He plopped her down on the tabletop, trapping her between his arms.

"You did something," Mitch accused her. "You look far too happy with Nick the Noodge being promoted."

"Of course I'm happy. I'm the one who gave the final glowing reports that got him his wish."

"You didn't." Mitch leaned in closer. "Why the hell did you do that?"

Anna lifted a finger in the air, her delight all too clear. "His promotion came with a transfer. This way he's out of our hair, and you'll no longer be tempted to run him over every time you see him."

A seed of satisfaction sprouted. "I wasn't tempted to run him over—that must have been *your* fantasy. I wanted to haul him behind the station and decorate his face with my fists."

"Wait for it." She held up a second finger. "And since Nick was so looking forward to being promoted for political gain, it's only right that he's now stationed in Hay River on the edge of Great Slave Lake. It's not as remote as what I first suggested, but it is one of the coldest stations in all of Canada. Does that make the situation brighter?"

Satisfaction hit full bloom. "He's going to the Northwest Territories?"

How did she look innocent and mischievous at the same time? Anna answered him oh-so-seriously. "It's a great opportunity for both personal and career growth. I hope he enjoys it."

She laughed then, the sound rolling up from deep inside as she clasped his shoulders and pulled him in tight.

Holding her in his arms was so right. They could have lost this, but they hadn't. Mitch took control again, lifting her and settling her in his lap. Kissing her laughing lips, curling his fingers into her hair and letting happiness wrap around them.

When they finally came up for air Anna sighed, resting her head on his chest. "Revenge is a dish best served when they don't see it coming."

A new burst of laughter escaped him. "Remind me to never again piss you off. You're evil."

"Keep groveling, you're getting better at it," she teased. Anna slid her fingers down the front of his shirt. "You know, this might sound strange, but I've been wondering. You never told me why you chose chains for part of your tattoo."

Mitch eased back far enough he could undo his shirt buttons before replacing her hand. She stroked the markings on his chest as he spoke. "Chains can pull us out of trouble. Give us a better grip when the hill gets too steep or icy. They may seem to be holding us back, but they hold us together as well."

She looped a finger around one of them, then paused, leaning in closer. "Is that my name?"

He nodded.

"I'm a link in your chain. Nice one, Mitch Thompson." Anna nodded. "I like that."

Mitch took a deep breath and took the final step. "You think you can get your parking sign changed?"

She frowned, pausing in the middle of doing up his buttons. "Why?"

"Because it would look even better if *Coleman* was spelled T-H-O-M-P-S-O-N." He pulled a ring box from his pocket and offered it to her.

Anna accepted it, a deep flush rising to her cheeks as she popped the case open.

"Oh my God, it's beautiful." Deep red sparkled at them. Anna's hands shook as she stared.

"It's not typical." Mitch pulled the ring free and held it up. "It's like you. Amazing, and dazzling, and so fucking gorgeous, with so much fire inside that can't be hidden. Not from the people who know where to look. The people lucky enough to see the real you."

She made this little noise somewhere between a purr and a cry. It melted his every defence.

Mitch paused, took a deep breath. "I really do love you, babe. Heart and soul. With every part of me."

She held out her hand and he slipped the ring on, wondering how in the hell he'd ended up doing such an old-fashioned thing. And yet it was the most right thing in the world to be doing.

Anna swallowed hard. "You're serious about getting married?"

"Hell, I just offered you a ring, offered you my name, and you ask if I'm serious. *Really?*"

She crawled off his lap only far enough to straddle him, looking him in the eye with joy on her face. "I love you, Mitch. I want to be with you, whether that's with the fancy fixings or without. But if you want to make it official, hell *yeah*. I'll marry you."

Mitch caught her lips and kissed her. Passionately, but tender. As if the fires they had between them were held back for the moment, never extinguished.

She rested her forehead against his. "You're amazing."

"I'm yours. That's what makes me amazing."

Anna kissed him briefly before leaping to her feet and backing toward the lake. "So. We need to celebrate."

Mitch followed after her, wondering what she was up to now. "It's still June, babe. If you're about to suggest we go skinny dipping, you're a few weeks early and half a mountain too high."

She pulled her shirt free from her pants. "How about tag then? First one to catch me gets to have his wicked way."

Mitch glanced at the empty parking lot then back at the trail leading into the bush before leering at her. "I have zero objections to fucking you against a tree. I'll give you a five-second head start."

She twirled and ran, her laughter rising to the heavens. Mitch waited long enough to ensure she'd be within the trees before he caught her. While chances were extremely remote, they didn't need to end up starring in a YouTube video made by someone who happened to drive past.

He took off after her, running smoothly, happiness and excitement both at an all-time high. Maybe this wasn't a typical way to celebrate getting engaged, but what about them was typical?

Mitch had the feeling he was going to spend the next fifty years chasing Anna. Which was only fair.

She'd caught him first.

I hope you enjoyed Mitch and Anna's story.

Sign up for my newsletter for the latest news on releases, free vignettes featuring past heroes and heroines, and other fun updates.

You've just read the first novella in the Thompson & Sons series. The full list of books in the series is Rocky Ride, One Sexy Ride, Let it Ride and A Wild Ride, all coming in 2014. There's also a bonus book, Baby, Be Mine, that's available now. That's Katy's story (the lone girl in the Thompson family).

If you'd like to post a review for this book, I would appreciate it. Reviews help other readers know if the story is one they'd enjoy.

You can also find me at:

My website, http://www.vivianarend.com

Facebook: https://www.facebook.com/VivianArend

Twitter: https://twitter.com/VivianArend

VIVIAN AREND has been around North America, through parts of Europe, and into Central and South America, often with no running water. When challenged to write a book, she gave it a shot, and discovered creating worlds to play in was nearly as addictive as traveling the real one.

Now a *New York Times* and *USA Today* bestselling author of both contemporary and paranormal stories, Vivian continues to explore, write and otherwise keep herself well entertained.

12703284R00099

Made in the USA
San Bernardino, CA
24 June 2014